Anisett Lundberg

CALIFORNIA, 1851

by Kathleen Duey

Aladdin Paperbacks

First Aladdin Paperbacks edition June 1996
Copyright © 1996 by Kathleen Duey
Aladdin Paperbacks
An imprint of Simon & Schuster
Children's Publishing Division
1230 Avenue of the Americas
New York, NY 10020

Designed by Randall Sauchuck
The text of this book is set in Fairfield Medium.
Printed and bound in the United States of America
10 9 8 7 6 5 4 3 2 1

Library of Congress Cataloging-in-Publication Data
Duey, Kathleen.
Anisett Lundberg / Kathleen Duey.—1st Aladdin Paperbacks ed.
p.   cm.—(American diaries ; #3)
Summary: The small piece of gold which Anisett carries in her pocket causes grave danger for her family living in the rough world of the California gold camps.
ISBN 0-689-80386-9
[1. Gold mines and mining—Fiction. 2. California—Gold discoveries—Fiction.] I. Title. II. Series.
PZ7.D8694An   1996
[Fic]—dc20
96-1393

It is late. Mother will notice the candlelight soon and tell me to sleep, but I must write or burst. Something has happened which could change everything. I found a promising rock last Sunday morning, wading the creek. I have hidden it since. I wish Pa was here. I must tell someone. I must find out if it is as good as I suspect. I know I should tell Mother, but she will want to make the claim, then sell out to some company or partnership and move us back to the states. Or perhaps she would want to work it, then go back to Indiana when it played out. I want to stay here, close to Pa's grave and the meadow and Deeker's Creek. Mother has talked about leaving since Pa died. This place isn't her home—she says so often enough. But it is mine, and Colin's.

Pa said that someday the gold will all be gone. When that day comes, we can raise cattle and farm and this place could be what my father wanted it to be—if Mother will stay. And she might if there were money enough to buy cattle, to hire hands.

There is another problem—the biggest one of all. If what I found is real, we will need partners for the heavy work and to keep the claim safe from jumpers. Mother always says none of the miners is to be trusted. Back in Indiana we had dozens of relatives and neighbors and friends. I was eight when we left, but I remember. We have no friends here. Mother talks to no one except old Schalt and Yen. If Pa were alive, he'd know what to do. I surely don't. Who can I tell? Who can I trust?

CHAPTER ONE

Anisett Lundberg woke in the dark. She could
hear the steady patting sound of her mother
kneading biscuit dough. Today would be biscuits
and gravy and probably stew. Anisett swung her
feet to the floor and stood up, rising to her tiptoes
to lift her petticoat and chemise from the wall
hook. Shivering into them, she pulled on her
dress, fastening it with trembling fingers. She
could feel the small stone in her pocket, bumping
against her thigh. She pulled her diary from
beneath her pillow and slid it under her mattress,
almost to the wall. Now more than ever, she did
not want her mother to read it.

Anisett spread her blanket over her bed, smoothing the tattered blue wool. Then she sat on the edge of her mattress, the pine needles and corn husks rustling as she bent to lace her right shoe. Pulling on the left one, she wriggled her toes, positioning the wad of newspaper that covered the hole in the leather sole.

Once she was dressed, Anisett faced the little window her father had made for her. It was real glass, not just oiled paper. You could see right through it. Outside the sky was flushing with dawn, rose and gray, the clouds frayed by wind. She lifted her mattress far enough to see the edge of the red tooled leather diary. It had been given to her mother by her grandparents to record the journey west. Her mother had never used it, so she had given it to Anisett. Anisett lowered the mattress. She'd have to find a better hiding place. Maybe the root cellar. But then she wouldn't be able to write every night as she did now.

Anisett touched her pocket and sighed. Time to get to work. She pushed back the blanket hanging across her doorway.

Anisett's mother was at the stove; her mother was always at the stove. The coal oil lamp sat on the table, making a yellow-orange globe of light in the middle of the room. It was warmer in the main room. Anisett stood, letting the softer air seep into the worn cotton of her dress. It was chilly. Maybe it would be an early winter. Anisett took a single step on the plank floor, and her mother spoke without turning around.

"Get the stew started."

Anisett crossed the room, glancing toward the alcove that served as her mother and brother's bedroom. The big bed was neatly made. Her brother was still asleep on his rope cot, his curly hair tangled on his pillow. He turned over restlessly, squirming into a new position. No one ever made Colin rise before daylight.

Anisett was immediately ashamed of her resentment. She loved Colin, but he acted like such a baby, always singing or playing with a stone or a leaf. He was so shy that he barely spoke to anyone. The miners made fun of him. Colin hated most of them.

Anisett pushed away the uneasy tightness in her stomach. The miners' teasing was rough sometimes. But Colin was fine. He was only eight and small for his age. He wasn't stupid, no matter what anyone thought. He would grow up this year. Then he would help with the work.

"Here." Anisett's mother's voice was brisk. "You might as well eat first." Startled out of her thoughts, Anisett took the chipped blue bowl and sank onto the hard bench by the table. The mush was yellow-white. Steam curled upward, touching her face. It disappeared when she blew on the hot cereal; then, as she inhaled, the steam pushed upward again. For a second, Anisett watched it rising, tumbling back on itself like the creek's current striking a rock.

"Stop daydreaming." Her mother's voice was terse. Anisett nodded without looking up and blew on the thick cereal again. She wished for honey or even blackstrap molasses to sweeten it. But honey was all for the miners now. Sixteen dollars a pound. An ounce of gold. Back in Indiana honey was sold for a few cents a pound, her mother said. But then, men back in the states worked for a dollar a day or less in wages.

"We'll do seventy supper pails today," her mother said quietly. Anisett looked up and her mother's voice rose. "Eat. There's work."

Anisett took a bite of mush. There was always work. Colin had shifted in his sleep again. Now one of his feet stuck out from under the blanket.

"Anisett."

Anisett lifted the spoon and blew, then lowered it back into the mush and stirred. "I have to at least wait until it won't burn my tongue," she murmured, then held her breath. Her mother leaned to pick up the cleaver, then began a steady chopping. She hadn't heard. Anisett was almost halfway through before her mother glanced around again, frowning. Anisett ate faster. The knock on the door startled her into looking up.

"About time," her mother said. Anisett got up to look out the peephole in the heavy cabin door. Yen had thrust his face close to it the way he always did. She could see his crooked smile and the sculpted plane of his smooth cheek.

"Morning, morning," he said through the door. He held up a plucked chicken and swung it back and forth.

"Let him in," her mother said.

Anisett lifted the heavy bar and pushed the door outward. Yen stepped high, dancing back out of the way, then reappeared, swinging the chicken again at eye level for her to appreciate. "Fat. Good." He grinned. "Yen always, always have best." Anisett smiled back, looking past him. Jai sat on the wagon seat, holding the reins, waiting for her father. The big bay geldings were restless, tossing their heads, eager to get on with the day's route. Anisett waved. Jai lowered her eyes shyly. She was beautiful, womanly, even though Anisett knew they were about the same age. There was something in the Chinese girl's quiet manner that Anisett envied. It was impossible to imagine Jai being clumsy or silly.

"Not always the best, Yen," Anisett's mother said sternly, wiping her hands on her apron as she came across the room. Yen ducked his head respectfully, bending just a little at the waist. The miners had just about teased him out of actually bowing to people.

"Best," Yen said firmly, lifting the chicken again. He glanced back out the door at his daughter on the wagon. There was rarely anyone else on their little road, but Yen was a careful man. He was smart, too. Instead of fighting against the feeling that foreigners shouldn't be allowed to work their own claims, Yen had switched over to selling supplies. Now he let the rest of them break their backs shoveling sand and gravel into the long toms and cradles. He drove a fine wagon to Sacramento City for picks and blankets and pans, and raised chickens and ducks and fat white pigs and got paid in gold.

Anisett watched her mother pinch the chicken's breast. Yen had presented it for inspection with a courtly manner; it was fit, his posture implied, for an empress. Anisett's mother lifted her fingers, playing her part, her chin regal, high. "You have more?"

Yen nodded tentatively. He turned to look at his wagon again, his long braid swinging. "Some," he said finally. "Not too much. Some."

Anisett watched her mother frown, not answering, letting the silence settle and stand between herself and Yen. Yen shifted his feet once, then again. Finally, he folded his hands and stared at nothing. He did it for so long that this time Anisett's mother was the one to move uncomfortably. "How much for this one?"

Anisett looked from her mother to Yen. His eyes narrowed. "Six dollar."

"Six?" Her mother's voice was faint with shock and dismay.

Yen's lips barely moved; his teeth didn't part. "Four dollar for you. Gold."

Anisett's mother wiped her hands on her apron and turned back toward the sink. Yen let her get halfway there.

"You buy ten, three dollar each."

Anisett watched her mother turn. "And pork? What do you have this morning?"

Yen ducked respectfully, once, acknowledging that the price of chickens was settled for the day. He ducked once more, to change the subject. "I have sardines. Twelve dollar."

Anisett watched her mother figuring. Tins of sardines could be sold at sixteen dollars or even more. But most of their customers were in the middle of a long day's work. They wanted to buy a cooked dinner and get back to their digging. The sardines could best be sold evenings in the camps, and Anisett knew her mother would never go into Morgan's Fork or Irish Crossing after dark. Too many of the miners were drunk then. Drunk and fighting, or sobbing for sweethearts they'd left behind.

"No." Anisett saw her mother sigh, giving up the idea of profit without work. "Pork?"

Yen half bowed. "Three dollar each pound."

Anisett stepped back to look out at Jai again. This time Jai waved. Anisett turned to see her mother frowning, but it took her a second to realize it was for her. "Stew." Her mother gestured with her chin.

Anisett walked to the drain board and dipped her mush bowl full of water. Once it was rinsed and dried, she set it back on the shelf. She took a kitchen bucket off its hook. Yen stepped aside, smiling and nodding as Anisett pushed the door open wider and went out.

Outside the sky was brightening and the

ragged clouds lying along the eastern horizon were fired into pink and rose. Anisett half turned, thinking that her father would love this sky, that he should see it. Then she stopped, unnerved. How could she forget, even for a second, that he was dead?

Anisett made herself walk on, rounding the corner. Well, it was true. Her father would have loved this sky. *Would have loved*. An ache pounded low in her stomach, then rose to beat in her throat. She would never stop missing him. It seemed as if her mother already had. She never cried anymore. She never talked about him. Neither did Colin—but then he had been four when they had come from Indiana and five when their father had died.

Anisett's grandparents—the whole family—had objected to her father's decision to take his family west. They had been afraid of the risk. The wagon train *had* been hard. They had been tired and cold and hungry for so long.

Anisett stared at the sky. The pink was giving way to a golden orange. Yen's wife had come from China with him. And his eldest son, who was about nineteen, and Jai. Anisett had seen a hundred Chinese miners. Like the Americans, the French, the Mexicans, the Chileños and all the rest, almost none had brought their families with them. What made Yen different? What had made her father different?

Anisett primed the pump, then set to work, lifting and lowering the long handle. Once the clear water had filled the bucket, she gripped the wire bail, leaning back against the weight. When she turned, pink and gold flashed within the circle of the bucket, the water reflecting the sky. She set it down, watching the reflected sky shiver with tiny ripples from the shock.

Anisett wondered when her mother would remarry. She had sworn she wouldn't until they got back to Indiana. The lonely miners tried to find a way into her affections. So far she had held them all at a distance—literally. She never told any of them where the cabin was. She distrusted them all, she said. They were all the kind of men who would run after a dream. Like my father, Anisett thought.

"Anisett?"

It was her mother's voice, piercing the wall, sharpened by criticism.

"Anisett?" This time her mother's voice was almost shrill.

"Coming!" Anisett hoisted the bucket and hurried back around the corner of the cabin. She didn't look at Jai, sitting primly on the wagon seat. It was embarrassing to have her mother scold her in front of visitors. Anisett set the bucket on the kitchen floor and grabbed another.

"Don't dawdle," her mother said as Anisett went back out the door. Yen was unloading crates of white plucked chickens. Jai was arranging crates behind the wagon seat. Anisett hurried to the storeroom built onto the back wall of their cabin. She lifted the bar on the heavy door and slid it sideways.

Once inside, Anisett let her eyes adjust to the dim light. In the center of the room a side of beef hung from a steel hook. It was lean and stringy, a steer her mother had bought from a desperate-looking man they'd run into on the road. Beef was rare north of Marysville and worth buying, even if it was fit only for stew.

The shelves along the rough storeroom walls held several hundred jars of applesauce. Anisett had peeled apples until her knuckles bled from the acid in the fruit. On Saturdays, her mother made desserts. If there were no fresh apples for pie, she made muffins with the apple-sauce. Muffins were two dollars each. The pies cost the miners sixteen dollars apiece. An ounce of gold.

Anisett glanced up at the bundles of drying herbs hung from the planked ceiling. Whatever wasn't eaten fresh from her mother's gardens ended up in jars or tied in little bundles to be used later. Yen's eldest son, and sometimes Jai, came to trade weed-pulling for cabbage or corn.

Anisett toed the little square doors set into the ground at the back of the storeroom, but she didn't open them. She didn't need to get into the root cellar. There were onions, carrots, and potatoes already in the kitchen.

Picking up the meat knife from its niche in the rough log wall, she cut long strips of meat from the flank of the beef, laying the pieces into her kitchen bucket. She would cut about fifteen pounds for a day's stew. Some of the miners would complain that it wasn't enough. Anisett smiled. Sometimes the miners offered to slip her gold for a pail with more meat. If only they knew how strict her mother was. She had to stir the stew between dippings, then lower the ladle no more than halfway into the pot. It was fair. No one got more than his share of the meat and vegetables. Or less.

"Anisett!"

The root cellar doors began to rise. Anisett realized Yen and Jai were gone. Otherwise her mother wouldn't have used the secret trapdoor set in the floor by her bed. It was hidden from strangers by a doeskin rug.

Her mother clumped up the rough steps, frowning, five butchered chickens swinging heavily from a line in her right hand. She tied the line to hooks set into one of the ceiling beams, then went down the steps without speaking. Anisett went back to cutting meat. A moment later she heard her mother come down through the trapdoor again; her next few footfalls were muted by the soft dirt floor of the root cellar, then got louder on the steps up into the storeroom. Anisett's mother emerged, carrying the remaining five chickens. She hung them, then let go. The chickens swung gently as she pushed a wisp of hair back into her bun. She looked tired. "All right. Let's get to work."

Anisett gathered the meat into her kitchen pail. "I'll get this on the fire."

Her mother nodded. "Do. Then wash vegetables."

Anisett looked back. At the bottom of the root cellar steps she could see two big baskets of apples. So. Yen had brought apples, too. That meant pies to bake on Saturday. The apples were very red and big. Anisett's mouth watered. She knew better than to ask for fruit while there was work to do.

"Hurry now," her mother said, swinging the cellar doors closed.

Anisett went outside, caught in an unwelcome rush of memory. The secret root cellar and the trapdoor had been her mother's idea—and she'd been right. It had saved them all during two attacks, one by Indians and another by bandits. But it couldn't save her father. Nothing could have. Cholera's swift and deadly fever had taken his life overnight.

Anisett walked back around to the front of the cabin, then set the bucket down on the porch. She crossed the yard and stooped to gather an armful of hay from the stack. She pitched it over the corral fence. Equinox brayed a greeting and thanks, a sound like rusty hinges being forced.

Anisett took a moment to rub the mule's velvet muzzle and ears. The clouds were deep gold now, the sun streaming around them, about to light the day. Equinox brayed his sunrise call, and as it faded to silence, Anisett's mother spoke from the doorway. "Anisett. Stop daydreaming."

CHAPTER TWO

Anisett finished making the stew and left it simmering on the fire while she washed dishes, filled the kindling box, then took the kitchen scraps out to the henhouse.

"Get that mule hitched up," Anisett's mother said when she came back in.

Equinox was happy to see her. She curried his rough coat and checked his hooves for rocks. The mule shifted as she worked the pick into the grooves around the sensitive frog of his hoof. Anisett slapped his neck. "Stand, Equinox.

Whoa." She softened the slap with a scratch behind the long floppy brown ears and leaned close to whisper. "Mother's hard to please today. Behave for my sake." Equinox blew a soft breath over her face. He smelled like sweet hay.

Anisett put the collar over Equinox's head, settling it over his withers. She ran her hand quickly around the underside of the leather, checking for burrs or harness tacks that had worked their way through. Then she buckled the collar and straightened the traces.

Equinox tossed his head. "I know," Anisett soothed him. "I know. But we have to." The mule snorted and Anisett laughed a little. "Complaints are useless," she told him, and eased back on the reins, walking beside him as she backed him into the wagon shafts. She picked them up, straining, and fit the near side into the leather boot. Then she circled Equinox, patting him to let him know what she was doing, and settled the other shaft. Equinox sighed as he felt the weight of the wagon settle on his shoulders.

"We'd better get going," Anisett's mother said from the doorway.

Anisett looked up, smiling at the pleasant tone of her mother's voice. Her mother was looking over her shoulder, talking gently to Colin.

Anisett snapped the crupper strap into place, stinging Equinox. The mule flinched and Anisett patted him, sorry.

"Let's get things loaded," Anisett's mother called. Her voice was all business now. After a moment she spoke again. "There's the oranges from Yen. I'm not sure how many to load."

Anisett was surprised. "I only saw apples."

Her mother arched an eyebrow. "You'd miss daybreak if Equinox didn't point it out to you." Anisett flushed, embarrassed. Her mother went on. "The oranges should sell for a dollar each. Or more. They all know oranges and lemons keep off scurvy. They learn it on the boats, if they didn't know it beforehand."

Anisett nodded. And oranges fit in a pocket, and the miners would want one for dessert or for dinner later. Fruit was scarce.

"Load a bushel," her mother announced. "Yen says most of them were freighted north of here. Maybe Schalt's or the wagon freighters running into Irish Crossing will have some. We'll know after today how to price the rest."

Anisett nodded. Her mother had already turned. "The other bushel," she said over her shoulder, "into the root cellar before we leave."

Anisett nodded, knowing her mother

couldn't see her. What would happen if she refused to work? She scratched Equinox's ears as long as she dared, then she started back toward the cabin. It'd be more fun if they did what Yen did—sold goods besides food. Yen's route varied every day.

Sometimes Yen went south after he left their house on Deeker's Creek and didn't visit the northern camps at all. Other days he drove southwest, back up the Yuba River to the Feather, sometimes as far as Sacramento City to meet the steamboats full of goods from Boston. Once or twice a year he took his wagon to San Francisco to buy directly from the ships that had come around the Horn.

There was a map in one of Anisett's father's books. When they had had their cookstove shipped from Boston, she had traced her finger along the route the ships took. It seemed an impossibly long way around South America then back up, half the world, almost, north to San Francisco. It had cost almost as much to have the freighters haul it to the cabin, but her mother figured she could sell it for a fortune when they left California.

Anisett put the extra bushel of oranges in the root cellar, climbing through the trapdoor and down the ladder slowly, resting the basket on each rung. She checked the storeroom's lock bar. Once raccoons had dragged meat and vegetables all across the yard.

When Anisett came in, Colin was at the table, eating his mush, his little blue bowl surrounded by rows of shiny tin lunch pails laid out and ready to fill. He looked up, still sleep-soft and rosy. She smiled and touched his hair, feeling a twist of envy. Colin wouldn't have to rush his breakfast.

The stew pot was sitting in the embers of the fire. Anisett took the pot rag off its high hook and raised the lid. Delicious steam made its escape into the room, and she hoped the Morgan's Fork miners wouldn't buy all the stew. When they made their dinner stop at Angel's Hill, sometimes there were only biscuits left.

"I've got the pails set out," her mother said from the doorway.

Anisett frowned. The pails were always set out by the time she got Equinox harnessed. Besides, they were plainly visible, spread across every table and bench and chair in the room. Yet her mother felt she needed to be told?

"Half with stew, half with biscuits and gravy," her mother was saying. "I'll do biscuits."

Anisett padded her hand with the pot rag to lift the stew kettle from the fire onto the hearth. The big ladle would fill two pails to the level her mother had decided was a fair meal for the three dollars they charged. Anywhere back in the states, people would laugh at that price. The miners paid it eagerly, measuring gold dust into paper tubes.

Anisett lifted the heavy ladle and, using the pot rag to catch droplets, carried it to the pails laid out on the kitchen table. She filled two, then crossed back to the hearth for more stew, stirring carefully and dipping from the middle. Her mother worked from the iron stove.

"Fill quicker," her mother ordered.

Colin smiled. His angel smile. "Can I take the reins today?"

Her mother nodded. "We'll see. If there's time." She glanced at Anisett. "We're a bit late."

Anisett turned her back. Why would they have less time today than the day before and the day before that? It hadn't rained since March. The roads were fine. The miners would take about the same amount of time to line up and buy as usual. There'd be time for Colin to play at driving the mule.

Unless, Anisett thought, I delay us somehow. Is that what Mother's saying to him? That I might take his treat away by being too slow? Anisett squared her shoulders and carried the ladle back and forth, stirring in fast, circular strokes. She dipped up the spinning stew, her skirt flaring out as she turned from the kettle to the pails, then back. She was on the thirtieth pail when her mother finished the biscuits and gravy and nodded brisk approval. Usually Anisett was much further behind.

Anisett finished the last five pails, coming out with less than half a ladle extra. She saw her mother nod again, and she hurried to split the excess among the lowest-looking pails. Then she carried a stack of lids from the drain board and began sliding them down tight on the pails. She turned to see her mother bending to kiss Colin.

"Run out to the wagon now. Here." Her mother handed him two lunch pails. "You can take these as you go." Colin took the pails solemnly, walking slowly, careful not to swing his arms. Her mother waited until he was out the door, then turned. "Let's load. Stew on the right."

Anisett nodded and set the pail handles upright, sliding her hand through the arched wires until she had five on each arm.

As Anisett stepped out onto the porch, the sun rose above the cloud bank, warming her face.

Equinox was standing with his head down so Colin could reach his ears. The old mule's eyes were closed in bliss as Colin scratched him, their faces close together.

Anisett walked to the side of the wagon and leaned over the sideboard, lifting both arms like a swimmer's stroke so the pails didn't catch or tip. She set them down, five at a time, slipping each arm free and straightening her back in one fluid motion. She arranged her second load of pails parallel to the first. Then she fit in the right side divider board to corral the pails and keep them from sliding. After her next load, she fit the wider center board into its slot, a notch chiseled into the base of the seat bench. Once it was secure, she went back in to get the remaining pails. She worked along the edges, sliding pails this way and that, fitting the extras in where she could make enough room. Her mother had finished the kitchen cleanup and had begun carrying the biscuit and gravy pails. Anisett hurried to help.

Colin stood quietly as they worked, his cheek on Equinox's shoulder. As Anisett hurried back and forth, she could hear him humming a melody that wandered in soft circles.

When Anisett came out carrying the cloth-covered basket of oranges, her mother climbed up into the seat, hoisting Colin up beside her. He sat on the wooden bench, his legs dangling down over the strongbox. Anisett checked the center board, then the dividers. She pulled her bonnet out of her pocket and put it on. Then she lifted her skirts and stepped up on the passenger pegs, swinging her leg over the sideboard just behind the bench. The cheese crate that served as her seat creaked as she put her weight on it. Today, the basket of oranges was jammed in, so she placed her feet carefully to keep the basket from grinding against her leg.

Her mother felt under the seat, checking the rifle. Then she smacked the reins across Equinox's rump. He shifted his weight and flicked an ear. She snapped the reins again. Equinox sighed and leaned into the collar, testing the weight and balance of the load. Finding it no worse than usual, he set off, slow and steady. Her mother glanced back. "Tell me if you see loose lids."

Anisett nodded. She would. She surely would call out if any lid had the audacity to work its way loose. Her mother turned back to face the narrow, uneven road that lay before them.

Anisett watched the lids carefully at first, flickering her eyes across one row of pails, then doubling back to follow the next row as the wagon slammed and tilted across the deep rut at the end of their lane. They made the slow, steep turn onto Deeker's Creek Road and headed east. Anisett kept checking. The lids were all tight. None leaked.

Anisett began to relax a little, loosening every joint in her body so the lifts and sudden, jolting drops of the wagon passed through her without hurting. After a long time she allowed herself to touch her dress pocket and felt the little yellowish rock, warm and solid. Everything was going to change. Everything.

CHAPTER THREE

Anisett had closed her eyes, letting the sun flash and fade against her eyelids as they passed beneath the pines. Her mother was humming, something she did to pass time and whenever she was thinking. The wagon jolted. Anisett opened her eyes. The morning sunshine splintered as it fell through the boughs, bright shards that made her sit up straighter. Colin was riding along in silence, smiling to himself. Sometimes Anisett wished for a brother who made noise and caused trouble.

Anisett twisted around to see the road ahead. Endless tall pines framed the rutted track as far as she could see. She heard a hawk's scream and looked up. For a second the bird was visible, its flight smooth and silent. Then it was gone.

Anisett stretched her legs, moving with the sway of the wagon. She touched her pocket. She wasn't sure how to stake a claim, wasn't sure a girl could do it at all. Maybe the smartest thing was not to tell anyone. She could go look again whenever she had time. She smiled, liking the idea. Every week or two she would find another nugget, and in a year or so, she would show her mother. Then they'd be able to buy fine cattle and clear some of the forest to plant corn. Maybe they could build a better house. That might make her mother happy enough here to want to stay. Other families would move in eventually. Then she could have friends and parties, like the girls she had read about in old copies of *Harper's* that Mr. Schalt saved for her. Back in the states, there were schools for girls.

California was a state now, too, Anisett reminded herself. It had been for months. Everyone had been so excited when President Polk had signed the Compromise. But nothing had changed, really. Nothing felt different to Anisett. Every month more miners came, and they were making everyone a lot of money. Schalt said it could go on for decades like this. Others argued that it could play out at any time.

Anisett's mother was staring straight ahead, her eyes darting from one side of the road to the other. Theft was always a possibility, Anisett knew, and there was the loaded rifle within easy reach of her mother's right hand. But a bandit with any intelligence at all would wait until they were on the way home with the day's gold.

Anisett straightened, easing her back, then slouched again. How much money would be enough? Her mother said they'd never have an opportunity like this one again. It was probably true.

Anisett watched her brother swinging his feet in rhythm with Equinox's swaying gait. His rosy face was solemn. Anisett pushed her hair back beneath her bonnet, uneasy. It was hard to imagine Colin grown up. She tried to picture his face with a beard, rowdy and loud like the miners, or even quiet and somber like the Mormon Camp men with their big families. She shook her head. It was impossible. Colin turned and gave her his angel smile, and she grinned back at him.

Her mother half turned, her face softening as she saw Anisett grinning at Colin. For a second Anisett's mother smiled at her. Then Anisett blinked, dazzled as a sudden opening in the trees let the sun gild the shadows, hot gold through the cool green. The wagon hit a rut, tilting, then righting itself as Equinox's plodding carried them back into the shade. Anisett looked; her mother's smile was gone.

"I want to hurry through the Morgan's Fork bunch. No waiting while they wash pails. And don't get Finlay started. That man will talk all day." She turned back to face the road, flicking the reins over Equinox's rump.

Finlay likes you, Anisett thought. They all do. She looked at her mother sitting, straight and capable, on the hard wooden driver's bench. Any man would want to marry her. She could do any kind of work, she could take care of herself, she was a good cook, and she was pretty. Anisett touched her own face. They didn't have a mirror, but once or twice in the creek she had found still enough water to see her reflection. Maybe she was going to be pretty, too. Maybe.

"Anisett." Her mother's voice startled her. "Did you hear?"

Anisett struggled to recall what her mother

had said, automatically scanning the pail tops to make sure nothing was loose.

"Did you hear?"

Anisett gave up the pretense. "I can't remember what you said." Her mother jounced the reins. Equinox flicked an ear.

"I said," Anisett's mother began slowly, "we want to hurry through Morgan's Fork. No waiting. They either have the bucket clean or they pay the extra dollar."

Anisett nodded, then realized her mother couldn't see her. "Yes, Ma'am."

Anisett's mother twisted around to look straight into her eyes. "And I don't want to take time anywhere else, either. The days are getting shorter, and I'd like to get close to home before it's pitch dark."

Anisett nodded. That meant no time at Schalt's to talk or look at magazines or the old copies of the San Francisco *Picayune*. Her mother turned back to the road, transferring the reins to one hand so that she could tousle Colin's hair.

Anisett stared out the back of the wagon as the walls of green pine slid slowly past. Her hand stole into her pocket. Her thoughts swirled like fish at the bottom of a creek, circling, passing each other over and over. Anisett shifted uncomfortably on her crate. She checked the pails, running her eyes across the lids. None loose. Her thoughts circled again. She would find out first. If it was real gold, she would tell her mother.

"Adams & Company," Colin said, his face coming alive. "I hear them."

Anisett listened. She couldn't hear anything over the hollow clopping of Equinox's hooves. But she trusted Colin's ears. He had turned all the way around on the seat, his feet poking her in the back. He leaned to whisper in her ear, his thick hair smelling like clear creek water. "Behind us." He gave her a confident smile. "Coming fast."

Anisett doubled at the waist, leaning toward the rear of the wagon. She heard her mother make a small disapproving sound in her throat. "The lids . . . ?"

"Are fine," Anisett answered quickly, straining to hear as she ran her eyes over the rows of pails, hoping she hadn't lied. She hadn't. She exhaled and closed her eyes, concentrating. Finally, like a thought rather than a sound, the faint jingle of harness rings filtered in through Equinox's clopping. "Now," Anisett announced. "I hear them now."

Colin shook his head solemnly, but his eyes

sparkled with laughter. "That's awful. I counted to fifty."

Anisett nodded, smiling at him. Fifty was Colin's all-purpose large number. All numbers over ten were fifty to him. Anisett resolved to try harder to teach him to count. Someday, somehow, he would have to learn to figure. How else would he know if someone was trying to cheat him?

The distant jangling of harness fittings came closer, accompanied now by the muted drum roll of hooves. Anisett smoothed her hair, tucking the wisps that had blown free back under her bonnet, glancing to make sure her mother didn't notice. She didn't want to hear her mother's lectures on men just now. She was only twelve. Most men didn't notice her at all. That didn't mean she didn't care how she looked.

All at once, the six-horse coach burst around a bend about a quarter mile behind them. Anisett's mother glanced back, then pulled the reins sharply, so that Equinox angled, clopping his way to the extreme right side of the road.

Anisett heard the shouts of the driver, though she couldn't make out the words yet. The special messenger, his rifle across his knees, sat on the second seat. Up front, with the driver, a passenger rode, one hand up to steady his hat against the rush of air from the thunderous speed of the coach. Anisett had never seen a woman ride up top, but she wanted to someday.

"Run, you devilish sons of heathen monsters," the driver bellowed, pulling the team gradually wider, taking a line on the other side of the road without slowing their headlong gallop.

Anisett looked forward at her mother's stiff back. Her mother hated it when the coaches passed them like this. It scared her. She was white-faced now, Anisett knew, but her hands were steady as she tugged Equinox a little farther to the side, risking sinking the wheel in the soft shoulder of the road.

"Watch it up now! Watch it, you godforsaken clumsy-hoofed, thick-skulled, rope-eared offspring of sway-backed devils," the driver bellowed. Anisett smiled. He knew her mother was driving and that she and Colin were there, or the curses would likely have been far worse. She recognized him. He was a handsome dark-haired man with clear calm eyes and a reckless tilt to his hat. He held the horses steady, nodding and touching his hat brim respectfully as the coach passed, dust and small rocks churned into the air by the galloping team.

Through the coach window, Anisett got a

glimpse of the passengers. A gray-haired gentleman in a good suit sat next to a rough-looking man with a huge black beard. Their ages and differences wouldn't matter much in a week or so, Anisett knew. They'd both be stooped and muddy from shoveling tons of sand into sluices or long toms or cradles—or they'd be sore and sick from squatting with a pan in an icy creek twelve hours a day. They'd have that strange, unhappy light all the miners had in their eyes.

Not very many miners struck it big. Most of them struck nothing at all. Anisett's mother said that was why they drank so much, had so many fistfights and gunfights. They were all crazy, according to her. Sometimes Anisett thought her mother was right. She had seen men bloody each other's faces over imagined insults, unproven theft—and sometimes out of sheer boredom. The grinding labor and frustrated dreams of their daily lives were hard on all of them.

Anisett suddenly pictured a hundred men swarming over Deeker's Creek and her father's pastures like ants on a honey dish. She shivered. They would if word of her find got out.

The wagon jolted Anisett from her thoughts. Inspired by the passing of the coach, Equinox had arched his tail and broken into a trot. Her mother slapped the reins across his rump to keep him at it as they rounded the bend. They were almost there.

Colin's face, enraptured as the coach passed them, had gone still, expressionless. He gripped the edge of the seat. Anisett reached out and squeezed his shoulder. His muscles had tightened into knots. He really hated going into the camps. Too many of the miners had made fun of him.

Anisett slid her hand into her pocket. The little stone rolled into her palm, and she closed her hand around it. Maybe she could get Colin a tutor, someone who would know how to help him learn. Then no one would make fun of him anymore.

"Stop daydreaming," her mother said without turning around. "Fix your bonnet."

Automatically, Anisett reached up to straighten the ties beneath her chin, then ran her finger just beneath the rim to push her hair under.

"Morgan's Fork," her mother announced like an Adams & Company whip, lowering her voice to a mock growl. "Proud location of three cabins. Four if you count the one that's fallen down. And a dirt floor boardinghouse equal to any grand hotel north of the Yuba River. Get on, now,

Equinox, you swift-footed, sweet-breathed son of a prancing dandy."

Anisett giggled and her mother threw her a conspiratorial grin over her shoulder. Then Anisett saw her mother glance at Colin's tense form and the rare smile vanished. Anisett's laughter seemed out of place, and she looked past Colin, wishing she could somehow make everything easier for him.

Ahead of them, the rough cabins and tents of Morgan's Fork were arranged in a crooked semicircle. Miners were crowding around. They stood, dusty and exhausted, shifting their weight uneasily as the driver handed down bags of mail to the man with the rifle. Starved for news from loved ones, the miners were always desperate for letters. Anisett watched as one man shoved another and shouting broke out.

"Morgan's Fork," her mother said again. This time her voice only sounded tired.

CHAPTER FOUR

"Mister, I don't think you heard me," the driver was saying calmly as Anisett's mother pulled Equinox to the far side of the clearing, then to a stop.

"Don't move yet," her mother cautioned, and Anisett glanced at her brother. Colin still looked frightened, but some of his tenseness had gone. It was obvious the miners were too preoccupied to tease him today. His wide eyes were fastened on the dark-haired driver. Anisett knew Colin liked him. The driver always smiled at him.

The crowd around the driver was a rough, muddy-shirted ring. Within it, a blond man with a drooping mustache stood wide-legged and angry. His hair was so light it was almost white. The mustache was the same color. He was sunburned, a boiled, painful red. His right hand hovered above the revolver tucked under his belt.

The driver faced him. "If you'll get in line, I'll see if you have mail." The other miners were sorting themselves into an eager queue.

The blond man stared. "I heard you," he began, his hand resting on his gun.

The driver took a deliberate step back and leaned against the coach, holding the mailbag. He smiled. "Everyone else here is likely getting tired of waiting for their mail, too, Mister." The driver's voice was pleasant, reasonable. "And I can't sort it until you take a place in line." The driver gestured, carefully keeping his hand away from his own gun belt. "Aren't you boys tired of waiting?" His voice was genial, light.

The driver pulled out a single letter and held it up. The effect was magical. The men hushed and stared at the letter, trying to read the name of the lucky recipient. Abruptly, the blond man stepped forward and snatched the letter. The crowd was stunned, then voices rose in protest.

A big man with torn clothing shouldered his way forward. "I got a sweetheart letter in that bag. If that's it," he gestured at the letter crumpled in the blond man's hand, "you'll be sorrier than you can imagine, friend."

The ragged miners shuffled their feet and cleared their throats. The line they had formed began to dissolve, reshaping itself into a ring about the blond man. The driver glanced around the clearing, and Anisett felt his eyes cross her face, then stop on her mother's.

"Well, now. Dinner's here," the driver said. His voice carried in the tense silence. Anisett glanced up. Her mother's eyes had narrowed, the tiny wrinkles that touched the corners tightened, but her posture remained straight and assured as the men turned to look at her. Then she spoke. "Won't you please just hand the letter back?"

The blond man swung toward them at the sound of a woman's voice. He squinted, leaning forward, as though getting a few inches closer would allow him to focus on her face across the clearing. He was obviously surprised to see a woman in the camp. His mouth puckered up, then relaxed as though words had been taken from him. He looked like a fish with a drooping blond mustache.

Anisett glanced at Colin. He pursed his mouth, then let it go slack, imitating the blond man. Anisett held her breath to keep from laughing. Colin made the fish mouth perfectly. He pushed his lips out, then opened his mouth wider, working it open and shut as the blond man had. An instant later Colin's snorting, helpless laughter rang out in the clearing.

"Don't." It was a hissing whisper from their mother.

Colin's eyes went blank at her fierceness. He slumped over in the wagon seat, his cheeks and ears bright pink.

"You. Boy!" The blond man was staring at Colin. "What are you laughing at?"

Oblivious to how silly he looked, he made the fish face again, waiting for Colin to answer. Colin began to giggle, his hands over his mouth. Anisett hushed him. Her mother bent to whisper something in his ear.

Anisett glanced across the clearing. The blond man had stiffened with rage, his hand on his gun. Anisett felt what was left of her own laughter fall backward into fear. The blond man pulled his gun from his belt, and the voices of the miners around him were swept into silence. For a second his gun rested on Colin; then, as the man turned, it swung with his motion.

Instantly, the driver let the mail sack fall, his own pistol drawn. Seemingly unaware, the mustached man kept turning, the gun pointing vaguely at chest level, moving slowly across the gathered crowd. Some men stepped back, pushing those behind off balance. Others stood their ground and drew their own weapons.

"Get down," Anisett's mother commanded. "With Colin. Behind the wagon."

When Anisett hesitated, frozen by her own fear, her mother reached out and grabbed her shoulder, her hand as quick as a thought. "Go." Anisett hurried to the rear of the wagon to scoop Colin up, then ducked back, sinking down behind the buckboard.

Colin squirmed against her as she waited for the sound of gunfire to drown the clattering rush of her own heart. Instead, she heard her mother's voice.

"Mister, if you'd put that gun away, I would be very grateful."

Anisett struggled to keep Colin in her arms, but he spilled forward, crawling beneath the wagon. She grabbed his ankle, terrified, but he lowered himself to the ground, belly down, and closed his eyes. Anisett tried to pull him back, but he had gone limp. This was one of his oldest tricks. She squeezed his ankle, digging in her nails, but he didn't respond at all. She knew from long experience that when he got like this, he could lie still without reacting, without even seeming to breathe.

Desperate to get him back behind the wagon, Anisett wriggled down beside him. "Look," she whispered, shoving her hand into her pocket. "Look at this. Colin. Colin?"

He opened his eyes and blinked, slowly curling himself around. She pulled the stone from her pocket and handed it to him. "It's gold, I think. I found it."

Colin sat up, and she pulled him toward her as he turned the stone over in his hand. "Gold?"

Anisett quickly touched his lips with her forefinger, shushing him. "Yes. But don't tell anyone. Not even Mother. Not yet." She rocked him a little as she shifted him across her lap and set him on the dry grass behind the wagon. Equinox stamped flies off his hind foot and Anisett flinched.

The silence was too complete. Colin was playing with the little stone, rolling it in his hand, turning it to see it shine. Anisett ducked to look beneath the wagon, out across the clearing. The first thing she saw was her mother's clean, frayed skirt hem. The cloth was vibrating. It took Anisett a second to realize that it was her mother's trembling fear setting it in motion.

Anisett squeezed her eyes shut. The guns would start any second. She wanted to shout at her mother to get down, to run. But what if her voice startled the gunman? Seconds ticked past. The silence seemed sharp now, as piercing as a scream. Anisett stretched to see. The crowd of men had opened up a clear path between the blond man and the wagon.

Anisett saw her mother's skirt flare out suddenly as she took a step forward. "Now, gentlemen. There's mail to sort and there's stew and biscuits and gravy. Put your pistols away." Her voice carried easily in the quiet clearing.

Anisett held her breath. The men were glancing at each other, then back at the blond man who held his gun loosely now, as though he'd forgotten it was in his right hand. The letter was crumpled in his left. Equinox stamped a front hoof, then, a second later, he snorted and shook his head, the harness jingling. The common everyday sounds seemed to soothe the harsh silence, smoothing its edges.

The blond man shoved his gun back beneath

his belt, muttering something Anisett couldn't hear. One by one the other pistols disappeared. The dark-haired driver stood without moving until the last one had been holstered. Then he raised his hand, gesturing at the letter. "If you'll get into line—"

"There won't be one for me. Never is," the blond man cut him off. Then he flung the crumpled envelope in the dirt and wheeled around, picking his way through the crowd. Anisett scrambled to her feet. Colin stood up beside her, still playing with the little piece of gold. Anisett took it from him, gently. "I'll let you see it again later," she whispered.

The blond man paused at the far edge of the clearing and glared back over his shoulder at Colin. Instinctively she put her arm around him.

"Anisett. Let's get on," her mother was saying, her voice tight. Anisett began collecting the clean pails from the miners who were lining up to buy. The talk was muted; the men seemed especially polite.

"I have oranges today," her mother announced, and a murmur ran through the line as Anisett uncovered the basket. She looked up after she folded the cloth, scanning the clearing. The blond man was gone.

CHAPTER FIVE

Even Equinox seemed glad to leave Morgan's Fork. After a half hour on the road, Colin had relaxed. He was playing a game with his hands. It took Anisett a few minutes to realize he was following the rhythm of Equinox's clopping hooves.

"I want to get through Angel's Hill as soon as we can. Then Irish Crossing and home again. I don't want to be on the road tonight after dark."

Anisett nodded. The pines were spooky after dusk. Once they'd seen a mountain lion. It had screamed like a creature from hell, its eyes shiny in the moonlight. Her mother had shot the rifle into the air and scared the lion off, but Equinox hadn't stopped shaking until they turned onto their own little road. Colin had curled into a ball and lain in the wagon until they had gotten to the cabin.

"I hate dark," Colin said quietly to himself, but Anisett heard. So did her mother. They both reached to touch him and their eyes met. Anisett's mother looked away quickly, not speaking until she had turned back toward the road. "You're good to him. A good sister."

Anisett didn't know what to say. She waited for her mother to turn around so she could smile at her, but she sat straight, the reins draped over her hands as Equinox clopped steadily onward.

Colin went back to his finger-counting game. Anisett shifted on her cheese crate, thinking about the stone in her pocket. Most of the miners had partners. It was impossible to work a long tom or a sluice alone. But who? She had to find out whether her little rock was gold—and how pure it was. Some claims yielded only a little low-grade gold and were abandoned. Who could she ask?

"Your father would be very proud of you. The way you help." Anisett's mother spoke as though she were addressing the road ahead of them.

Shaken from her thoughts, Anisett stared at the pine trees. Her eyes stung. She fingered the little stone in her pocket. She should tell her mother. But when she opened her mouth to speak, she couldn't. Instead, she pressed her lips together, wishing her father were alive. Her stomach tightened as the wagon pitched high on one side. Her mother and Equinox sometimes disagreed on the best way to negotiate a deep rut; their compromises were often the worst way.

"Lids," her mother reminded tersely.

Anisett ran her eyes over the shortened rows. "Fine." Her mother did not answer, and the hollow rhythm of Equinox's hooves went on after they had lurched up out of the rut.

Angel's Hill wasn't on a hill. It was set in a narrow valley, with a road cut into the hillside above the little river. Coming around a curve, they met two men on horseback. Both tipped their hats, politely trying not to stare, just as most of the miners did. Any woman was a curiosity.

Once they were past, her mother slapped the reins on Equinox's rump. "They need wives. Wives and sweethearts and sisters and mothers."

Anisett looked up to see the two men turning a bend. One of them looked back and she quickly looked aside. He was handsome, and his saddle and horse looked fine. Maybe he'd made his pile and had bought them from one of the Spanish Californios' enormous ranchos.

"Angel's Hill," Colin sang out suddenly, half standing like the dark-haired driver always did coming into a camp. He pretended to crack a long whip. Anisett laughed and her mother smiled. Equinox shuffled into a jog-trot. Angel's Hill was his dinner stop. His oat bag was under the seat.

Anisett's mother pulled Equinox to a stop in front of the two-story building that served as store, hotel, and saloon. The trough, filled with cool, mossy water, drew Equinox's attention, and he sank his muzzle in it, swallowing noisily as the line began to form.

"Good day, Mr. Schalt," Anisett heard her mother greet the portly store owner. Schalt had haunted the stream beds, finding carpenters and skilled mill hands who hadn't found enough gold to turn down his offer. In a month Schalt had one of the best buildings in the northern gold fields outside the bigger towns like Stockton or Sacramento.

By the time the rains had started, he'd established his rooming house upstairs for miners who wanted to stay close to their claims through the floods—or to keep poking around the hills for digging sites. Downstairs, he'd had the carpenters build an elaborate bar, with mirrors above it that he'd had shipped from Boston. Anisett's mother shook her head as she always did, looking at Schalt's building. "And what happens to him if Angel's Hill plays out? Most of them do."

Anisett nodded. It was true. The miners would hear of a rich find thirty miles away, or ten, or a hundred, and they would desert their camps overnight—leaving a dirty scatter of torn tents and rusting tins behind. The shopkeepers could only hope the tide would turn, or pull up stakes and follow. Schalt had too much invested in his building to do that now.

Anisett's mother swung down out of the seat and handed Anisett the oat bag. Equinox eagerly pushed his muzzle into the bag and had eaten half the oats by the time she had buckled the headstall behind his ears.

While her mother banged the wooden gate open, Anisett helped Colin find a spot on the far side of the wagon where he would be hidden from the miners who were appearing from all directions.

"Clean pails, here," Anisett called out, stationing herself as always at the rear of the wagon.

Her mother worked from the side with a stick into which she'd driven a long nail.

"Biscuits and gravy," the first man said, and her mother reached across the wagon bed, extending the stick to hook a pail handle. She lifted it gracefully and swung it around. The miner took it from the nail and handed her mother a little packet of gold dust. Anisett turned back.

"Good morning, Miss Pretty." Anisett recognized the man. He had been at Irish Crossing before coming here. He was nice, a friendly sort who would probably never even make back the passage he had paid to get here. His friendliness always drew a frown from her mother. Today he was rewarded with more than that.

"My daughter is here to work, not to make conversation," Anisett's mother said sternly.

The man ducked his head and smiled at Anisett, winking sidelong. Anisett glanced at her mother. She hadn't seen. Anisett was glad. Her mother would have refused to sell him a supper pail. When Anisett didn't react to the wink, the man moved on to the front of the line.

"Here, Miss," the next man said, removing his hat and making her a bow. Anisett nodded politely. His front teeth were missing when he grinned. She pulled the lid off his clean pail, tossing it into the oak bucket already half full of lids. Then she stacked his clean pail with the others, keeping her eyes on her work.

"How do I purchase a meal?" the next man asked, and she looked up at him. He was young, eighteen at the most, dark-haired and brown from the sun. His face was unfamiliar, and his clothes were almost clean. He smiled at her pleasantly. Anisett glanced at her mother. She was frowning.

Anisett nodded briskly. "Just buy a dinner pail today, and when you want another, bring the pail back clean. If you do, it's three dollars. Without a clean pail, it's four. A quarter ounce, gold." Anisett waited for him to argue. He was new enough to think the prices too high. She looked at his boots. The dark leather was muddy, but unscuffed. His hands weren't calloused. Definitely a newcomer, and he had come by ship. The men who came overland looked hard and weathered. "Where are you from?" she asked impulsively.

"Is it that obvious?" He smiled. "New Hampshire. My uncles are out here somewhere. Place called Irish Crossing. You know it?" The next man handed Anisett a clean pail and the line moved forward. She nodded, pulling the lid off and stacking the pail. "Just north of here. We go there after this."

The young man nodded courteously. Anisett watched him as he paid her mother. He was awkward at tapping the gold dust into the paper tube to measure it. At least he'd been smart enough to change whatever money he had into gold before he'd come to the camps. A lot of the storekeepers wouldn't honor paper currency from back in the states. Her mother sure wouldn't. The young man walked away, glancing back once.

Anisett recognized the next miner. He had been in Irish Crossing all summer, a quiet older man who coughed and looked exhausted all the time. Did he have a claim here now? He handed her a clean pail. Anisett started to pull the lid free, then looked down at it. The lid was bent.

"I reckon your ma won't give me the full dollar off?" The man looked earnestly into her face.

She shook her head. "Probably not."

He grimaced, looking down at his feet. "I've seen the elephant," he whispered, using the miners' expression for losing their dreams of wealth. "I guess I'm about to go home, if I can raise the fare."

He looked so sad. Anisett resisted an impulse

to pat his shoulder. "I won't tell her about the lid," she whispered between her teeth. His head jerked up. "Just go on." Anisett glanced at her mother.

The man smiled at her. "Thanks, Miss. I won't forget it."

Anisett took the next man's pail, then the next's, covering the bent lid in the bucket with theirs. Her mother would be angry but not that angry. The pails cost less than the dollar deposit she charged, and lids were cheaper yet.

The next man in line had been drinking, but he remained polite despite the whiskey fumes surrounding him. Anisett almost gagged when he leaned toward her to explain that his clean pail was in his tent. He pointed grandly across the clearing, a sweeping gesture that took in half the state.

"Bring them both tomorrow," Anisett suggested. "And we'll put both toward your dinner pail then." He smiled crookedly and with an exaggerated drop of his shoulders, sighed.

"For a month I haven't gotten anything for my back-break but sparks and chipsa."

Anisett nodded to show she knew what the words meant—finding chipsa was worse than finding nothing. The fine dust made many men keep digging the same claim, hoping the gold would coarsen into grains and pellets, which added up quickly enough to make one hundred dollars a week, the minimum amount needed to keep them from moving on. But chipsa didn't always mean bigger gold. Often, the gold played out entirely. The hard part was deciding when to quit a claim. Sometimes someone else came along and washed another ton of gravel and sand in the same spot—and struck it rich. Anisett thought about the gold in her pocket. Would she be one of the lucky ones?

The man was still staring at her, his face a mask of dejection. Anisett pointed firmly toward her mother. "Please. You're holding up the line, Mister." He nodded as though he was just remembering where he was.

"No pail," he said as he turned, and Anisett relaxed. Sometimes the men tried to cheat. She hated arguing with them when they had been drinking. It was always better during good weather when they could work every day. The miners drank more during the long wet winter when they had little to do but sit in their rooms, or worse, their tents.

Many of the miners left the fields altogether when the rivers rose and the skies threatened. Some went to Sacramento City or San Francisco.

Others, like Schalt's tenants, prospected in the hills, away from the rivers.

The next man in line handed Anisett a clean pail and she stacked it, then glanced around. Colin was playing quietly, singing one of his breathy, wordless songs.

The line of men kept coming. So many of them bought oranges, she wondered if she should hide one for herself and Colin for tonight's supper.

Anisett's mother was all business, moving the miners along like reluctant cattle. They all wanted a word with her, a smile, a few minutes of feminine company. Her voice cool, nearly stern, she gave them their dinner pails, took their money, and that was that.

"That brother of yours is a strange one, isn't he?"

Anisett turned to face the next man in line. He was big, at least six feet tall, and his face was innocent, interested. He watched Colin intently, then he looked up. "I got a cousin acts like that. Something ain't right. Sweetest-natured kid you'd ever want to meet, though."

Anisett lifted her chin, pretending not to hear. The man shook his head. "I didn't mean to offend. He just reminded me of my cousin, that's all."

When Anisett still didn't answer, he shrugged and went on toward the front of the line. Colin glanced up at her with a strange expression, and Anisett wondered if he'd heard. "We won't be too much longer," she assured him. "Equinox could use an ear scratch, I bet. And his oat bag needs to come off."

Colin got up and dusted off the seat of his pants. He stood for a few seconds, plotting a course to the front of the wagon that wouldn't take him too close to any of the miners. Equinox lowered his head as Colin got close. Colin raised his arms as Equinox leaned toward him, a little dance of friendship.

"I want a dinner pail."

Anisett looked up and her heart beat so heavily that it hurt. It was the blond man. Up close, even his eyes were pale and cold, the icy blue of melting snow.

CHAPTER SIX

"Do you have," Anisett began, then her voice failed and she had to start over. "Do you have a clean pail?" She glanced at Colin. He had moved almost beneath the wagon. Only his elbow and a triangle of his jacket showed.

The man squinted. "Clean? What?"

Anisett explained. The blond man listened, his head tilted theatrically, as though he were fascinated with every word. When she had finished, he shook his head with exaggerated dismay. "I have no pail, clean or filthy. I never bought slop from you before."

"My mother is a good cook," Anisett said automatically. The man chuckled. It was a cramped, humorless sound. Anisett couldn't smell whiskey on his breath. But if he wasn't drunk, what was wrong with him?

Anisett's mother gave the blond man a pail and took his measure of gold without speaking. Her face was set, expressionless, as though she didn't recognize the man at all—although Anisett was sure she did. His white-blond hair was uncommon, and his strange, angry eyes were unforgettable.

"Thank you very kindly," the man said, a parody of politeness. A sarcastic smile twisted his lips.

Anisett's mother nodded curtly. Instead of leaving, the man looked around at Colin. "Nothing making him laugh now?"

Anisett's mother did not answer.

"That's a shame. No more jokes?"

Colin sat motionless, his eyes downcast. Anisett was afraid to move, to breathe. Abruptly, the blond man turned away, walking across the clearing in front of Schalt's store. He disappeared around a corner without looking back.

"I hope we don't see him again," Anisett's mother said quietly. Anisett nodded, looking at

Colin. He was humming to himself. Anisett took a deep breath and turned to the next man in line. He was gray-haired and grizzled, impatiently proffering a clean pail. She took it and waved him on.

Anisett concentrated on making the line diminish, taking the pails quickly. When the last man had gone, there were only seventeen pails left. Colin crawled out from underneath the wagon and went to pat Equinox. "Yen is coming," he said.

Anisett smiled. "Is he?"

"We are going to start making eighty or ninety pails," Anisett's mother said as she opened the strongbox and put the paper tubes of gold dust inside. "We could probably sell a hundred some days. Angel's Hill has grown."

Anisett nodded, her heart sinking. It already took her almost two hours every night to wash all the pails and dry them. If her mother didn't stop increasing the number of dinner pails, they were going to have to stop sleeping in order to keep up. Anisett's mother was beaming.

"Imagine it. Three hundred dollars a day! Not all profit, of course. Meat prices keep going up. Maybe we could plant a bigger garden." She smiled, her face bright and animated.

Anisett tried to look enthusiastic. "That would be wonderful."

"Yen's here," Colin said clearly.

Yen and Jai sat side by side, not talking. Yen held the reins. He grinned when he saw them. Jai tipped her head a little. As they got closer, Anisett could see her smiling—just the corners of her mouth turned up, her posture perfect, hands gracefully folded in her lap.

Schalt appeared in his doorway. He bought merchandise from Yen and resold the goods to the miners at a profitable markup. Yen never sold directly to the miners at Angel's Hill. It was part of his arrangement with Schalt.

"Gather up," Anisett's mother said. "We can wait and eat our dinner at Irish Crossing." She glanced around, and Anisett knew she wanted to avoid the blond man.

Anisett turned back to her work. Twice she caught Jai glancing at her. They were probably the only two girls within fifty miles, Anisett thought suddenly. Maybe a hundred. There were some families in San Francisco now, Yen had said. But after last January's floods, men would think twice about bringing their wives and children upriver to Sacramento City. Next year they might.

Or maybe, Anisett thought, there wouldn't be a Sacramento City at all by then. Whole camps disappeared overnight. When the gold was gone, the miners might just all go back to wherever they had come from. Anisett wondered if her father had been right. Would California turn into a rich, settled place, with towns and cities? He had believed it when he'd brought them here, and he had died believing it.

Anisett felt the familiar aching just behind her eyes. She moved the remaining dinner pails close together on one side of the wagon, resetting the divider to separate stew pails from biscuits and gravy. She glanced at Mr. Schalt, standing beside Yen's wagon, dickering over prices.

Anisett smiled to herself. What would it be like to have gold of her own to spend? Schalt's store was full of picks, gold pans, riveted canvas trousers, and skillets—miner's supplies. But there were stores in San Francisco that had anything anyone could ever want. Or at least that was what Yen had told her in his singsong English. "Many, many thing, all kinds. Whole world bring."

"Stop daydreaming."

Anisett looked up at her mother. "It's ready. We can go."

Colin perched on his side of the wide board

seat. Anisett pulled her cheese crate closer to the center of the wagon, where the jarring was slightly less than directly above the front axle. There was room now. Too much room. With only seventeen pails left, they would run out at Irish Crossing, leaving some customers without a meal. Anisett hoped there wouldn't be too many arguments over a place in line.

"Wake up, Equinox." Anisett's mother pulled the reins in little tugs until Equinox backed up a few steps. Once there was enough room to turn, she shook the reins.

Anisett looked back as Equinox leaned hard into the traces to get the wagon rolling, then ambled in a wide semicircle. Yen came out the front door of Schalt's, carrying an empty packing box. Colin called out a greeting and Yen grinned back. Jai smiled her little half-smile. Anisett waved as Equinox pulled them steadily past, back out onto the narrow road.

"Hoofbeats," Colin said after a few moments. "Adams & Company." Without a single second's hesitation, Anisett's mother pulled Equinox at an angle, jigging the reins over his rump to hurry him along. They got to the far edge of the road just as the dark-haired driver whipped his team around the curve. Colin beamed and

Anisett saluted him, smiling. He was so proud of his excellent hearing.

Once they were back on Deeker's Creek Road, Equinox clopping along, Anisett scooted her cheese crate sideways, to let the sun warm her back. She squinted up at the sky. It was afternoon, probably about one o'clock. It would take about two hours to get to Irish Crossing. She let her thoughts drift, watching the pine trees creep past the wagon, her whole body swaying with the jolting of the wooden wheels.

About halfway to Irish Crossing, Colin tilted his head. "Someone's behind us. Just one horse."

Anisett looked back, uneasy. They had never been robbed, but more and more stories about bandits were being told. Her mother leaned down and pulled the rifle from under the wagon seat. She handed the reins to Colin. He held Equinox on a steady course while his mother checked the rifle breech to make sure it was loaded. Then she laid it across her lap and took the reins again. "Closer?"

Colin tipped his head again. "A little. Not going very fast."

"See anything?"

This was directed at Anisett. She had been trying to spot the rider, but the road was curved here, winding its way between the mountainsides, following a stream that fed into Deeker's Creek just above Angel's Hill. "No. Too many bends. I'll keep watching."

"Do," her mother said uneasily. She slapped the reins across Equinox's back until he reluctantly began to trot. It was a futile gesture, Anisett knew. Any man on any horse could easily overtake a wagon pulled by an old mule.

They came to the upgrade that preceded the final set of hairpin curves leading into Irish Crossing. Equinox slowed to a flop-eared walk, hauling the heavy wagon up the steepening road.

"Closer now," Colin said. "And there's another one, I think." His voice startled Anisett, and she felt her heart speed a little. Colin had heard people behind them a hundred times, and it had always turned out to be someone they knew or some stranger who only doffed his hat at the sight of a woman, then rode on. There was no reason to think that this time would be any different.

Anisett stared at the road behind them as Equinox pulled the wagon higher and higher. There. She could see a rider now, on a tall sorrel with a wide blaze down its face. As she watched, the rider turned in the saddle and waved. "I see someone," she said. "He's waving." For answer, her mother only clucked at Equinox. It's because of the blond man, Anisett thought. He's the reason we are all so edgy. She squinted to see the rider clearly. He had on a hat. She couldn't see the color of his hair. As she watched, the man waved a second time and spurred his horse into a canter.

They were past the top of the grade when the rider came loping up behind them. "Do you know him?" Anisett's mother asked over her shoulder. Anisett started to say no; then she hesitated. She did. It was the young man with the new boots. He waved and she waved back. "Yes," she told her mother, relief in her voice. "It's that newcomer— the young one from New Hampshire."

"Thank God," Anisett heard her mother murmur. Colin wriggled around on the seat to look back. His face was pale. Anisett could feel her own heart thudding. They were all being silly, she thought. Sometimes the miners shot each other, it was true, or started fistfights that spread through their own camps. But no one had ever tried to hurt Anisett's family. The miners were almost all honest men who worked hard—too hard—under terrible conditions. Anisett watched the young man approach. After a year of stooping over in icy water ten hours a day, then sleeping wet in a filthy tent, maybe he would look like the rest of them—grizzled and tired and bitter.

"I thought it was you folks," the young man called out as he got closer. His voice was so friendly that Anisett realized all at once how lonely he was, how far away from home. He cantered even with the wagon, touching his hat respectfully. "I'm on my way to Irish Crossing, too," he said cordially.

Anisett's mother nodded. "It's a good camp. They've had a couple good strikes lately."

Anisett watched her mother, astonished. She rarely chatted with the miners. Maybe it was because this one was so young.

"Where's the other one?" Colin asked so quietly that the young man frowned, leaning toward him.

"Pardon me?"

"Where's the other one?"

Anisett remembered what Colin had said, but the young man only looked puzzled. "Maybe you were wrong," she chided Colin. He shook his head, then looked down, withdrawing into himself. Anisett saw the young man staring curiously at Colin. She squirmed on her cheese crate seat. Colin needed to learn to stand up straight and shake hands and look people in the eye. People would notice him less if his manners were better.

As they followed the dusty road, the young man introduced himself as Tobias Gleason. "Mrs. Rosa Lundberg, Anisett and Colin Lundberg," Anisett's mother responded. They all smiled and rode in amiable silence for a time. Then, the young miner tried talking to Colin. After a few attempts, he got a shy answer. Anisett saw her mother watching, her eyes soft, almost friendly.

The miners at Irish Crossing were already lined up by the time Equinox shuffled around the last curve. Because the camp was on a steep hillside, the road stopped short of the actual tent town at its center. A web of paths led from the valley floor up to the camp, and a few late miners were making their way down them now, lining up at the last wide bend of the road. They had learned from long experience that Anisett's mother was not about to go traipsing among the claims with a covered basket of food.

Reputations aside, the camps could be very dangerous for a woman alone. For anyone alone. Anisett had heard of miners getting sick and dying if they had no friends to bring them food and make sure they were warm and dry. Anisett looked back at the young man who rode off to one side of their wagon. His eyes were wide, taking in the place, scanning the faces of the men in line.

"Anisett!"

Her mother's voice brought her back around, blushing. She had not really been staring at Tobias. But her mother was scowling at her. She sighed and adjusted her bonnet, looking at her feet until she felt the wagon lurch to a stop.

"There's the other one," Colin said softly. "It was *him*."

Anisett turned, then had to reach out to grab the wagon rail to keep her balance. The blond man was a little ways back on the road, slouched in his saddle, staring at them.

CHAPTER SEVEN

The blond man reined in beneath the branches of
an oak that overhung the road. His horse fidgeted, and he forced it around in a tight circle,
stinging its neck with the ends of the reins.

"Toby! Is that you? Almighty and all the
saints! It is! Toby!"

Anisett turned at the voice and saw the
young miner getting off his horse to run toward a
gray-haired man who was sliding down the last
steep section of the path. They embraced,
whooping. A third man skidded down the bank to

join them. All three slapped their hats against their thighs and laughed aloud, beaming at one another, talking all at once.

Anisett glanced back at the blond man. His face was indifferent; if he noticed her, or anything else for that matter, he gave no sign. Anisett tried to get her mother's attention, but she was watching Toby's happy reunion with his relatives. The two older men looked dirty and tired like all the miners, but their faces were transformed with grins of welcome. Anisett saw sadness and longing shadow her mother's eyes.

This reunion probably made her homesick, made her think of her own folks back in Indiana. She had left four brothers and three sisters—as well as her parents, aunts, uncles, and cousins— far behind in order to come to California with Anisett's father. She had always said they would go back as soon as they could.

Anisett glanced toward the blond man, pretending to bend to check her shoelace. He was gone. She straightened, scanning the road, the line of miners, the paths that snaked down the bluff. She saw a horse disappearing over the top of the ridge, but it was gone so quickly she wasn't even sure what color it had been. The blond man was nowhere to be seen.

"Did you see where he went?" she asked Colin. He shook his head.

"Let's get started," Anisett's mother prompted, finally looking away from the embracing men.

"He's here somewhere," Anisett said. She watched understanding seep into her mother's eyes.

"Where?"

Anisett shrugged and lifted her chin, gesturing. "He was over there, under the pine tree. He went somewhere while I was distracted by those three." She nodded toward the men who were a little quieter now but still patting each other's backs and shaking their heads in disbelief.

Anisett's mother glanced around the clearing, which was really no more than a wide spot in the road. The freight wagons and coaches had worn the turnaround wider than it had been for the first supply wagons, but it was still the end of the road.

"He must have gone up into the camp," Anisett's mother said. She reached up to smooth her hair, her eyes skipping across the line of men, then the paths on the bluff.

Anisett nodded. It made no sense to think he had turned back or just struck off into the woods.

Had the blond man been following them? Maybe he had held back because Toby had ridden with them. But what could he possibly want? She shivered, remembering his angry eyes. Surely he wouldn't hurt a little boy for laughing.

Colin was wriggling down off the seat. He usually stood by Equinox's head at Irish Crossing. There was no grass, nowhere comfortable to sit near the wagon, and he didn't like walking even a few feet away by himself. Equinox lowered his head for an ear scratch as Colin approached.

Anisett let down the back of the wagon and began taking the empty pails thrust at her by the impatient miners. Few took much of a dinner rest. Most ate quickly and went back to work shoveling and washing the streambed soil.

"Built a dam," one of the young miner's uncles was telling him as their turn approached. Anisett knew it was rude to listen, but she couldn't really help herself. They were standing less than six feet from her, and their voices were loud with excitement and their eagerness to share news.

"We've built a dam that diverts the water around a little bend, like a mill race, but it takes the whole creek aside. That leaves a straight section of dry riverbed." The gray-haired miner was beaming, delighted with the idea of tricking the river. "We're going to use river water from the dam pond, run it into a sluice, then down the long tom."

The young man shook his head. "What's a long tom?"

The older man gestured. "We'll be running the water through a wooden chute, see? Then we shovel the sand and gravel into the high end. By the time the water washes the dirt and light sand out the other end, most of the gold has sunk. You nail cleats in the bottom of the long tom to catch it up." He looked gleeful, but then he lowered his voice. "We've not found much yet. But we will. The little we've taken out has been high-grade."

Anisett glanced at her mother, who was accepting a paper tube of gold from the man at the head of the line. How was she ever going to find out if her gold was high-grade or not? Or if it even *was* gold? There were other minerals that deceived people. Maybe her find was really fool's gold—shiny but worthless pyrite or mica. If it was, all her dreams were worthless, too.

Anisett knew she couldn't go into Sacramento City to ask an assayer to look at her little yellow stone. She couldn't go anywhere at all except back and forth on Deeker's Creek Road.

Someone else might stumble across a nugget in the creek that ran behind their cabin, stake a claim, and the gold would never belong to her family. Taking a deep breath, Anisett pulled the rock from her pocket. For an instant, she just held it. Then she cleared her throat.

"Excuse me," she began, turning so that her body would hide the little rock from her mother's view. "Sir?"

The gray-haired man looked at her. "Me?"

Anisett nodded shyly, glancing at Tobias. They had called him Toby. He seemed honest and sincere—so maybe his uncles were good men, too. Anisett's palms were sweaty. "Don't make a fuss, please, Mister," she said as quietly as she could. "But would you look quick at this?"

The gray-haired man took the stone from Anisett's trembling hand and turned it over in his own calloused one. He looked for a few seconds into her eyes, then handed it back. "I would give a great deal to know where you found that."

Anisett stammered, then recovered herself and wrinkled her brow. "I was . . . I was just wondering if it was good."

The miner nodded solemnly. "I would say it's near pure. Very high-grade."

Anisett thanked him and quickly smiled her

gratitude, pocketing the gold. She nervously waved him forward, her heart beating with joy. He got his dinner pail. Anisett watched anxiously as he stood in front of her mother, but he didn't say anything, didn't betray her secret. She sighed in relief as he stepped back, waiting. The next man looked so much like him Anisett was certain they were brothers. They insisted on buying Toby a dinner pail. He let them, winking at Anisett when he told them he was mighty hungry indeed. She smiled back at him, sharing the joke, earning another frown from her mother.

"What's your name again?" he asked. "Anna?"

"Anisett." She felt herself blush and knew it was silly. He wasn't flirting with her. He was much too old to be flirting with a twelve-year-old girl.

"I appreciate your friendliness," he said earnestly. "Thanks for letting me ride along with you. I'll see you and your family tomorrow, I guess." He looked up with a grin so innocent and infectious that Anisett heard her mother exhale in surprise. "Nice to have met you, Ma'am." Then he looked toward the front of the wagon where Colin stood. "And good-bye, Colin." Anisett heard Colin murmur a response.

When she turned, Anisett saw her mother smiling at Toby. If he was half as good-hearted as he seemed and he worked hard, he would soon have more friends than he would know what to do with. He already had trusted partners in his uncles. Anisett envied him. He started up the hill with the two older men.

The line went quickly. They ran out of dinner pails and had to listen to the last dozen or so grumble and complain. Anisett's mother assured them that the following day there would be plenty for all again. "Angel's Hill is growing fast," she told them. "I apologize."

The men shuffled their feet but seemed appeased. The novelty of hearing Anisett's mother speak at all was something in itself. They stood and stared at her after she had finished, until she finally turned to Colin and told him to get back up in the wagon.

"Yen is coming," Colin said.

Anisett watched her mother nod absently, bustling around the wagon as the men finally walked away. "Tuck these up front," she said, handing the buckets of empty lids to Anisett.

Anisett laid the divider boards neatly into their slots, the spaces between them empty now. If they did start making eighty or ninety pails, they were going to have to figure out some way to load a second layer of them. The way the wagon lurched over the roads, it would be hard to prevent them from spilling.

Once the stacks of empty pails were arranged neatly just behind the seat, Anisett pushed her cheese crate next to them. Her mother was all business now, hurrying as she always did at the end of the day. They had at least five hours of Equinox's clip-clopping before they were home. They would be driving the last mile or so in the dark, but Equinox knew the road so well, and that last stretch was so flat and easy, it had never bothered Anisett before.

This evening, she was a little uneasy because of the blond man. But he was gone, she reassured herself. If he had wanted to make trouble, he would have done it by now. It was probably just a coincidence that he had come up this road at all. He was likely in Irish Crossing to see friends or to see if there was talk of rich new strikes, of men making their pile in some new area.

Yen's wagon came around the curve. He smiled and waved when he saw them. Jai waved, too, a small motion, her hand barely rising from the edge of the seat. Anisett looked at them, at the shiny stacks of picks and brightly colored blankets in Yen's wagon. The tins of sardines, in the wooden crates, were stacked along one side.

They ran into Yen at least twice a week now—he drove Deeker's Creek Road more often. There were enough men in the camps to make it worthwhile, even though Poker Flat, just below where Angel's Hill had sprung into life, had been abandoned.

Anisett noticed her mother glancing around the clearing. The blond man? Anisett looked up quickly. The clearing was empty except for a few miners who had seen Yen and were starting back down the bluff, calling to companions to sound the alert that Yen had arrived. Yen was grinning, no doubt happy that he had timed his arrival so perfectly. Now he wouldn't have to scramble up the steep path to tell the miners his wagon of goods was waiting below. Anisett saw Toby and the two older men turn and start down the path, too.

"Climb up," Anisett's mother called, and Anisett nodded, still looking at Yen's wagon and at Jai, who sat so straight on the front seat. Maybe someday she and Jai could talk. Jai spoke pretty good English—better than her father already, which was why Yen brought her along. But Yen always made sure she stayed in the background, waiting in the wagon, sitting silently until he needed her to help him translate a bargain.

Anisett's mother rapped the side of the wagon. "Anisett!"

She climbed in and adjusted her cheese crate so that she was facing straight backward. The blond man was probably up on the hill with friends, talking and joking. But just in case he started back to Angel's Hill and overtook them, she wanted to see him coming.

Equinox always clopped along a little faster on the way home than he did on the way out. As her mother eased the brake handle back on the downgrade coming out of Irish Crossing, Equinox broke into a shuffling trot to accommodate the easy roll of the wagon. The late afternoon sun was still warm.

"From summer straight to spring, then back," Anisett said aloud, echoing her mother's constant complaint about California weather.

Her mother turned and smiled. "And the winters are all rain and bluster. Never a good clean snow."

Anisett tweaked the back of Colin's neck. He squirmed, giggling. She tickled his ribs and he squealed in outrage and delight. She tickled him once more, then stopped, knowing it would make him cry if she kept it up too long.

Anisett's mother smiled at them, and then began to sing.

"Oh, don't you remember sweet Betsy from Pike?
Who crossed the big mountains with her lover Ike."

Colin and Anisett joined her to finish the verse, using Equinox's gait to time the music.

"With two yoke of cattle, a large yellow dog,
a tall Shanghai rooster, and one spotted hog."

Equinox tossed his head and slowed a little as the road flattened out and he could feel the weight of the wagon again. They kept the song going, changing to a slower rhythm to match his hoofbeats.

"Saying good-bye to Pike County
Farewell for a while,
We'll come back again
When we've panned out our pile."

They drew out the last word, then launched into the second verse. When the song was over, Anisett's mother began another, a new song that had gotten popular in the camps during the summer.

"Oh, what was your name in the states?
Was it Thompson or Johnson or Bates?
Did you flee for your life or murder your wife?
Say, what was your name in the states?"

Colin sang with her, loudly, mimicking the

miners' style of singing, raucous and a little off-key. The song was sung more and more often now. Everyone was saying it. Men who had no honest life in the states were beginning to arrive in California.

As Colin launched into a second performance of the song, Anisett thought about Toby. He was no criminal on the run from the law. And there were many just like him. Schalt was certainly honest. He had such a good reputation that miners often brought their disputes to him. He would figure out a fair solution and then everyone would abide by what he said, just like a judge. Colin let the last note of the tune fade and Anisett applauded him. He bowed, and Anisett's mother laughed aloud.

A sudden clatter of hooves behind them made Anisett jerk back around, taking in a quick breath.

CHAPTER EIGHT

The wagon jolted to a stop. Anisett heard her mother set the brake, then the click-*clack* of the rifle breech. As the hoofbeats got louder her mother raised the gun.

"Get down low, Anisett—both of you," she commanded tersely. Colin slid over the backboard and curled up beside the cheese crate. Anisett hunkered close to him but raised her head far enough to see. When the rider burst around the bend, he reined in, then saw the rifle and stiffened, pulling the reins high. His horse, a black with wide, nervous eyes, startled by the sudden appearance of the wagon in its path, reared and danced a circle. The rider hung on as the horse struck at the air with its hooves, but he lost his hat, baring dark hair and his open, astonished face. It was Toby.

"Lord God," Anisett's mother breathed. "That blond villain has me nervous enough to shoot a perfectly good boy."

Anisett straightened up. She tugged gently at Colin's collar. "Hey. It's okay. It's Toby. The one who rode with us up the Irish Crossing hill." Colin uncurled, his eyes wide. Anisett pushed his hair back on his sweating forehead.

"Might I ask why you are pounding up on us like that?" Anisett's mother inquired, holding the rifle out to one side, the barrel now aimed vaguely at the woods. Toby looked from her to Anisett.

"I was hoping to catch up with you." He patted his horse, loosening the reins so that it could stretch its neck, shaking its mane. "Uncle Jack loaned me his mare. They sent me with a message," Toby went on. He swung out of the saddle to retrieve his hat. He dusted it off, slapping it against his thigh. The mare startled again and he scolded her gently, holding tight to the reins. Then he looked up. He fixed his eyes upon Anisett. Suddenly her confusion lifted, and she began to understand. No. She didn't want this message. Not now. Not in front of her mother.

"Uncle Jack says if you want honest partners, to remember us." He paused. "You'll need men." He gestured at Anisett's mother and little Colin. "To do the work. It's heavy work, Anisett."

Anisett bit the inside of her cheek to still her tongue. Of course it was heavy work. Did he think he was telling her things that she hadn't thought of herself? How long had he been in the camps? A day? Two days? She glanced at her mother. The instant their eyes met, her mother spoke. "What is he talking about?"

Anisett didn't know what to say. Her mother looked more puzzled than angry. But how was she going to feel when Anisett explained that she had shown a complete stranger a lump of gold without telling her own mother? Her mother set the rifle back under the seat so that she could get down from the wagon. She paced, stretching her legs, then looked up. "I am waiting, Anisett."

"I didn't mean to start trouble," Toby said uneasily. He glanced at Anisett. "I surely didn't think . . ."

When he faltered, then stopped, Anisett's

mother turned, her head tilted to one side. "I am entirely at a loss, young man."

Toby looked helplessly at Anisett. It was clear from the unhappy expression on his face that he had no idea what to say or do next.

"Well?" Anisett's mother was only a few feet from Toby now. Anisett cleared her throat. All this was her fault, not his.

"I . . . ," she began, then trailed off. "I found—"

"Someone's coming," Colin said softly.

"Probably Yen," Anisett's mother said quickly. "As long as we have been standing here, he's caught up."

"Not a wagon," Colin said, tipping his head.

Anisett's mother turned to look at him. "Are you sure?"

Colin nodded. And then he pointed ahead of them on the road, not behind. "Coming from there."

Anisett felt herself relax a little. If the blond man came, it would be from behind them, not ahead. The tense wariness in Anisett's mother's stance softened. She started back toward the wagon, moving slowly enough to talk to Anisett over her shoulder. "I expect a full explanation from you."

In that instant, the rider came into sight. Anisett had no time to cry out a warning. The blond man came toward them with his gun already drawn.

"Well, then," he said slowly, his eyes moving from Anisett to her mother, then to Toby, then last, to rest on Colin's face. "Here we are." Anisett saw her mother ease toward the wagon.

"If you take another step," the blond man said evenly, "I will have to shoot."

Anisett's mother froze. "You can have the day's gold. It's in the strongbox behind the seat."

The blond man arched his eyebrows and let his revolver swing slowly to point at Colin. Anisett's mother drew in a quick, harsh breath. "He's just a little boy."

The blond man made a disgusted sound low in his throat. "And he ain't smart enough to ever be anything else."

"That's not true," Anisett's mother defended Colin.

"Close your mouth and don't move," the blond man said. "You." He indicated Toby. "Do you carry a gun, boy? Don't lie." Toby nodded slowly. "Give it to me."

Colin began to cry, a small sound, full of fear. The blond man glanced at him. "Quiet him down." He looked back at Toby. "The gun. Right now, and be careful. The little one here likes jokes, but I don't." Anisett put her arms around her brother as Toby opened his shirt and pulled a small shiny pistol from his waistband.

"A ladies' gun. Isn't that pretty?" The blond man chided.

Toby didn't answer. The blond man jerked his thumb toward the forest. "Throw it."

Toby sailed the pistol into the pines. Anisett heard it land. He had not thrown it too far. Toby's eyes grazed hers, then focused on the ground. "Now," the blond man said carefully. "Get into the wagon. Slow and careful. You don't want to startle me." Toby stood still, staring at the rutted dirt beneath his boots. His horse fidgeted, pawing the ground.

"I said you could have the gold," Anisett's mother repeated. Anisett could see her skirt trembling, the way it had that morning. The blond man laughed at her.

"So you did." He looked at his revolver. "This says I can have the gold if I want it. And I do, I do. But not just this minute . . ." He looked at Anisett's mother. "Just what is your name?"

She did not answer him. He swung the gun in the direction of the wagon. Colin whimpered, turning to Anisett. She tightened her arms around him. The man brought the pistol to a stop, pointing it directly at Colin. Anisett burned with helpless rage. How could anyone terrify a little boy like this? Would he shoot? What was wrong with him?

"Your name?"

"Mrs. Lundberg."

He clucked like someone correcting a stubborn child. "No. Your given name."

"Rosa," Anisett's mother said, her voice papery and dry. "My name is Rosa."

He lowered the gun. "Thank you, Rosa, for the offer of your day's take in gold. I am very grateful." He brought the gun back up and pointed it at Toby. "I said to get in the wagon." Toby held up his reins, arching his brows in question. "Tie your mare to the back," the blond man instructed. "And get *in*. I am not a patient man."

Toby walked to the wagon gate and looped his reins over the top rail. Then he swung one leg up and over. The wagon creaked and settled as he sat down and positioned himself so that he was between Colin and the blond man. Anisett shot him a grateful look.

"Now I will need that rifle, Rosa. Slowly and carefully."

Anisett watched the blond man slide her mother's rifle into a scabbard attached to his saddle. "Lost mine," he said, smiling at them. "In a card game when I first got here. Nice to have a rifle again." He patted the polished wood of the rifle stock. "Now, whip up that mule. We have quite a way to go, don't we?"

Anisett's mother looked at him sharply. "Where are we going?"

He laughed again and leveled the gun. "Go on."

She shook the reins. "Equinox won't go any faster if you point that at him," she said. The blond man didn't respond. The wagon creaked and began to roll. Toby's horse started forward when its reins tightened; its ears pricked up, amazed at the slow pace and the wagonload of people staring it in the face. Equinox humped his back in protest at Toby's added weight, but he went along steadily. The blond man dropped back far enough to keep an eye on all of them. After a few minutes, he began to whistle.

CHAPTER NINE

"Why are you doing this?" Anisett's mother asked after a long silence. The blond man didn't respond. She repeated the question. "You owe us that much."

He laughed bitterly. "I don't owe you anything, lady. I've been grubbing in the ground now for nearly two years. I've been sick, wet, cold, and dirtier than I ever was in my life." He looked heavenward like a man about to pray, then he cursed. "I've worked as hard as any man who lives in this hell of sand and rock. And I've found damn near nothing," he said, gesturing broadly enough to take in all the gold fields, north and south. "The hell with it all." He focused on Anisett. "I had about given up." She felt her stomach tighten.

"A lot of men are disappointed here," Anisett's mother said slowly, without taking her eyes off the road ahead of them. Anisett held her breath for a second. Toby caught her eye, his face tense.

"A man heard you talking to Uncle Jack," he whispered, barely moving his lips. "That's why they had me come. Irish Crossing was full of talk. They thought to be first to offer."

The blond man spurred his horse close to the wagon. "You got something to say, you best say it loud enough for me to hear it, boy. I saw you up at the camp on the hill. I know you think you got here first. It don't matter." Toby shrugged and looked away without answering. Colin made a tiny sound, and Anisett reached out to hold his hand.

The blond man reined his horse back, positioning himself where he could cover them all with his revolver again. "That one ought to be taught not to bother regular folks." He said it to no one in particular, to the sky, to himself. Anisett watched him in quick little glances, afraid to attract his attention but unable to look away.

Equinox's hoofbeats went on and on, a slow, rhythmic background for Anisett's racing heart and thoughts. For half an hour or more they rode along in a tense silence. "Adams & Company is coming," Colin piped up suddenly. His face was relieved, joyous. Anisett reached to touch his hand. He thought the coach coming meant they would be rescued. And it might have meant just that, if Colin hadn't announced it.

"Is it, now?" The blond man made his voice falsely cordial, warm. "Then I believe I will just ride down in the trees for a few minutes. But mind you," he said, and his voice dropped, "I'll have the gun on the boy the whole time. If that coach stops, he won't live long."

The blond man glanced toward the trees. The galloping clatter of the Adams & Company team was audible now. "I'll have the gun on the boy," he repeated, looking at Anisett's mother. "Keep the mule moving." With that, he spurred his horse over the embankment. It plunged and slid, disappearing into the pines.

A moment later the Adams & Company coach came into sight. Anisett tried to think clearly. She had to signal the driver—if she could just think of some way to let him know they were in trouble—without making him stop. The team thundered closer. The driver was yelling his usual stream of profane encouragement, popping the long whip.

Colin's face was strained, confused. He started to stand up. Anisett reached for him, but Toby was faster. Together they kept Colin seated, held his hands so that he couldn't wave at the driver.

Anisett's mother looked back twice, nodding grim approval when she saw that they had Colin under control. The seconds ticked past, slower than seemed possible. The coach approached them from behind, pulled even. The driver waved and Anisett's mother waved back. Then, the coach was in front of them. The passengers clinging to the seat that faced the rear waved at them, but Anisett's mother didn't bother to respond. The coach rumbled around the next bend and was lost to sight. Colin slumped and began to cry against Anisett's shoulder.

"It's going to be all right," she told him. "It is, Colin. Just be quiet and patient." She heard the tremor in her voice and knew he could hear it, too.

Colin leaned close. "I'm scared of him."

"I know," she soothed as the blond man whipped his horse back up onto the road. *Me, too*, she thought, without saying it aloud. *Me, too. And it's my fault that he's here at all.*

"Very good," the blond man congratulated them. "Except you," he said, pointing at Colin. "If you try to signal anyone again, I will—"

"He doesn't understand," Anisett's mother interrupted.

The blond man dug his spurs into his horse's flanks. The startled animal leaped forward, then plunged to a stop beside the driver's bench. The blond man stared into Anisett's mother's face. "I don't care how young he is, or how stupid. Tell him to sit still. This is my only chance."

Anisett watched the blond man lean out of his saddle and lash the ends of his reins across Equinox's rump. Equinox, startled and outraged, shuffled into a resentful, jogging trot.

"It's a wonder he gets you up the mountain at all," the blond man scoffed.

"He's old," Anisett's mother answered. "He serves us well enough and he's gentle—"

"When I want to hear the mule's history, I'll be sure to let you know." The blond man spat into the dirt. "Where did you find it?" He glanced up at Anisett and caught her eyes. She tried to look away and couldn't. When she didn't answer, he lifted the gun, aiming it toward Colin.

"Near our cabin," Anisett said.

He smiled at her, then turned. "How long before we get to the cabin?" he asked Anisett's mother.

Anisett could see her mother take a breath, then hesitate. After a few seconds silence, she answered. "We usually have to drive the last hour or so in the dark."

"The mule can just go a little faster this time, then." The blond man leaned out to whip Equinox with his reins again. Equinox shook his harness in protest. The man only laughed. "Keep up with that and we'll put the boy's horse in the traces instead."

Toby raised his head. "She isn't broke to harness. You'd have a bronco on your hands is all."

The blond man looked at Toby, a thoughtful expression deepening his eyes for a moment. "Bronco? You picking up the Spanish lingo already?" He rubbed his face with his left hand. "You know, nothing counts here. Not family or schooling or even hard work. Any lucky Chinaman or Mexican or some deaf ol' coot from New York who ain't got strength to lift a pick can strike it. Or some little girl—" He struck his saddle horn with his free hand. "But not me. It ain't right."

No one answered, but it didn't matter. The blond man rode close to Equinox again, slapping him hard with the ends of his reins. "I said, whip him up," he snarled at Anisett's mother. She jiggled the reins over Equinox's back, talking and clucking. The blond man watched her critically for a moment, then seemed to slump into his own thoughts again.

"If we could get him off his horse," Toby whispered, "I think I could—"

The blond man raised the pistol. Toby sat back. Colin began to cry again, quietly. Anisett slipped her hand in her pocket and felt the little lump of gold. It had changed everything. That part of her dream had come true.

"Yen and Jai," Colin sniffled. Anisett quickly hushed him. The blond man was riding alongside Equinox again, trying to keep him trotting. Anisett looked up the road. They were at the bottom of a long, gradual incline. At the top of the ridge, the rough track into Angel's Hill turned off. Equinox wasn't capable of pulling the wagon up it at anything but the ambling walk he loved best. Anisett's mother had told the truth. Equinox was old.

"Barely whisper, Colin. How close are they?" Anisett breathed into Colin's ear, pretending to hug and comfort him.

"Not too close. They're going slow," Colin answered, tickling her ear with his lips.

She squeezed him hard for a second. "Don't worry. Just keep quiet and don't make him angry."

Colin nodded and sat back. Anisett glanced up to find the blond man staring at them.

"Secrets?"

Anisett shook her head. "He's just frightened, that's all."

The blond man looked up the road, then behind them, before his eyes came to rest on Anisett again. "He might be smarter than I thought. Maybe he just plays stupid."

Anisett saw Colin duck his head. She wanted to hit the blond man, to knock him off his horse and make him apologize to her brother. Her whole body shook with fury. What gave him the right to insult Colin, to scare them all like this?

CHAPTER TEN

When they were about a half mile from the Angel's Hill cutoff, Yen and Jai finally came into sight. While the blond man was preoccupied with glancing behind, squinting to see who was in the following wagon, Toby leaned down to fiddle with his trouser cuff. "My uncles will come looking," he whispered.

Anisett watched the blond man out of the corner of her eye. He hadn't noticed. He had reined in, turning in his saddle to get a better view of Yen's wagon. He gestured at Anisett's mother, raising the gun. "Keep on just like you are."

Anisett's mother made a show of shaking the reins. The blond man looked behind them again.

"Your uncles won't know where we live," Anisett whispered back to Toby. "My mother never tells anyone—"

"Stop that," the blond man roared, spurring his horse so hard that the animal squealed as it wheeled around, its hooves throwing chunks of soil.

Anisett kept her eyes down, listening to the beating of her own heart. The blond man reined his horse around the back of the wagon, then spurred it again. Once even with her, he leaned halfway out of his saddle, the pistol weaving with the motion of his horse's gait.

"I want," he said between his teeth, "no more whispering."

"What do you expect from them?" Anisett's mother asked quietly, evenly. "You're scaring them. They are just children." Her voice broke a little on the last word, betraying her own fear.

The blond man forced his horse so close that Anisett's mother had to lean away when its muzzle grazed her shoulder. Its eyes were wide, rimmed with white, sweat darkening its shoulders. It wasn't from effort; the poor animal was terrified. The blond man had already hurt it, jerking the bit against its tongue. The foam from its mouth was flecked with blood. The blond man hauled on the reins again now, wrenching the horse away from the wagon. He looked back down the road. "Can't you make that damn mule go any faster?"

Anisett's mother shook the reins without answering. Equinox shuffled a little faster for a few steps, then slowed. "Well, they've already seen me," the blond man said, talking to himself again. He raised his head, pointing the pistol at Anisett's mother. "When they come up on us, you act like you would any other day. I'll say I am riding with you to see you safely home. And you'll smile nicely and agree to that."

Anisett's mother nodded. The blond man glared at Anisett. "You, too." She nodded. "And you," he spat at Toby. Toby nodded. Colin nodded without further prompting, his eyes wide and frightened. The blond man laughed his ugly, grating laugh. "Well, then, I guess we all agree."

Anisett shifted uneasily. Maybe Yen would figure it out. He knew that her mother never allowed any of the miners to know where she lived—much less accompany them home.

Anisett's mother had made strict rules when she had started the dinner pail business. If none of the miners ever came to their door, no one could gossip. Nor could anyone rob them. Once Yen had brought a starving miner to their door for a bowl of stew. Anisett's mother hadn't begrudged the man a free meal; it was his presence on her porch she was furious about. Yen had never brought another stranger.

Colin's sudden flinch bumped Anisett out of her thoughts. The blond man was brandishing his pistol again. "I don't want you to say anything to the folks in the wagon. Is that clear?" Colin started to curl into a ball.

"Just say yes," Anisett's mother prompted him, looking back over her shoulder. Her face was tense and bloodless.

"Yes," Colin managed. It was loud enough for the blond man to hear, and he nodded as though they had struck a fair bargain. He holstered the pistol, looking back over his shoulder. "Hell. It's the Chinaman, ain't it?"

No one answered and he didn't ask again. Once the gun was no longer aimed at Colin, Anisett looked down the road at Yen. Could he have seen the blond man pointing the gun? She squinted. No. She couldn't even make out Yen's hand on the reins yet. Or the color of Jai's blouse.

Yen and Jai gained ground simply because

Yen had two big bay geldings pulling a nearly empty wagon while old Equinox, pulling alone, had had his workload increased at the end of an already long day. They will pass us about where they always do, Anisett thought. It had never seemed that important to her, except as a chance to wave at Jai, to exchange a look with her and wonder about her life.

"No tricks now," the blond man said, glancing back. Yen's wagon was almost close enough for them to shout for help, Anisett thought. Yen's English was pretty good, but her mother sometimes had to repeat things to him two or three times. A quick shout might mean nothing to him. Even if he understood, Yen could hardly outdraw the blond man or overpower him. Anisett shook her head. Yen didn't even carry a gun, or if he did, he was clever enough to keep it very well hidden. A lot of the miners objected to anyone but Americans having guns—even the Californios, who had been here long before them.

Anisett glanced at the blond man. He focused on her and spoke as though she had asked him a question. "I aim to make a little luck for myself today. I told Lila I'd come back with a pile. She'll be sorry she didn't wait. 'Cause I *will*." The last two words were desperate. He stared at

Anisett, but she was pretty sure he wasn't really seeing her. She looked away and he didn't seem to care, or even notice.

Toby's horse had its head down now, bored with the slow pace and resigned to the dust from the wagon wheels. Anisett looked past it. Yen and Jai were getting closer. She couldn't risk trying to tell them directly that something was wrong. They might figure it out from Toby being in the wagon and the blond man's hovering presence. Or they might just think the blond man was courting her mother and Toby was his son, or hired help, or any of a dozen explanations. Would they even care?

Anisett stared, helpless, as the big bays pulled Yen and Jai closer. Once they were almost directly behind the wagon, Yen cracked his old buggy whip to move his geldings from a jog to a smart trot. Hooves hammering at the soft dirt road, the team swerved smoothly to the center of the road. Jai met Anisett's eyes as she always did: only for an instant, her gaze sliding away.

Help us, Anisett shouted inside her mind. *Help us! Go get Schalt or Toby's uncles. Show them the way to the cabin. Please, just help us.* Jai lifted one hand from its perch on her knee. The wave was small, barely noticeable, as always. Anisett fought hot, painful tears, unable to wave back. Yen drove his wagon past, nodding politely at her mother when they drew even, not looking back once they had passed.

Anisett wanted to scream. How could it be over so quickly? Their only chance of getting help was gone. Why hadn't she done something? Why hadn't her mother?

Yen and Jai were almost at the crest of the grade now, passing the road that led up the river to Angel's Hill. Couldn't they tell something was very wrong? She glanced at Colin. He looked ill and was practically lying down, for heaven's sake. Usually, when Yen drove past, Colin was up on the seat, begging to have a turn driving Equinox.

"Very good," the blond man said quietly once Yen's wagon had disappeared over the rise. "Let that mule stumble along as slow as he wants for a bit now." He took his hat off, then resettled it farther forward on his forehead. The sun had burned his cheeks and neck to brown. Where his hat rested, his skin was milk white.

Toby reached out to rub Colin's hair a little. Colin opened his eyes, startled. He closed them again, squeezing them tight. Anisett wanted to tell Toby that this was what Colin always did when he was frightened or upset. Anisett wondered what the blond man would do if Colin actually played dead as he sometimes did. He would not be likely to have much patience with Colin, that much was sure.

"How much farther?" the blond man asked.

Anisett's mother seemed startled, and she didn't answer for a long moment. He just stared at her, waiting.

"To our place?"

The blond man frowned. "Do you think I mean to San Francisco? How much farther?"

"About an hour and a half. Maybe a little longer," Anisett's mother answered warily, but it was the truth. The blond man shook his head.

"Won't that mule go any faster? Why don't you get a horse? Sell that rat bait to the Indians for stew meat."

"No!" Colin said, coming out of his silence.

"He doesn't mean it," Anisett said quietly.

The blond man nodded, an exaggerated, mocking gesture. "Yes, I do. The mule's barely fit for dog meat, but the Indians would take him. They're used to bad bargains. The Spanish rancheros don't give them anything fit to eat, or wear, either—they just work them all season, then run them off with a sick cow or a blanket for pay."

"That's no excuse to mistreat them further,"

Toby said quietly, watching the blond man's face intently.

"Well, well. You're green," the blond man scoffed. "Right off the boat and soft and stupid. Probably still have your copy of old Sherwood's *California and the Way To Get There*, don't you? Or did you bring *The Pocket Guide to California*? Or both? Neither one really says what a man is going to find here, does it?" He reset his hat.

Toby hesitated, and Anisett watched him. "I guess I have a lot to learn," Toby said cautiously.

The silence stretched out again. The blond man rode without saying anything for so long that Anisett found herself relaxing enough to feel weary. Colin had closed in on himself again. Probably the only thing that could have roused him was talk of Equinox being eaten by Indians. Anisett shifted her position, careful not to bump Colin. He was much safer withdrawn and silent.

"Let me see it," the blond man said suddenly, from right beside her. Anisett jerked upright, startled. His icy eyes were on her face, intent and excited. "No one else is likely to come down the road now. Let me see what you showed them at Irish Crossing."

"You might as well," Anisett's mother said, and Anisett could hear the anger in her voice.

Anisett hesitated. The blond man was watching her eagerly, fascination widening his eyes, like a man watching a horse race on which he has wagered everything he has left. Even his breathing had quickened. "Come on," he demanded, his hand on his pistol.

"Show him," Anisett's mother said flatly. "Do you want him to hurt us? Can't you understand what you've done?"

Anisett, stung by the accusation, reached into her pocket. She brought out the little stone and held it for an instant. Then she reached out toward the blond man. He stood in his stirrups and leaned to take it from her. Anisett felt her eyes ache, then flood with tears as he sat back in his saddle, turning the little lump of gold over and over in his hand. She had been so foolish. Her mother was right. This was all her fault.

CHAPTER ELEVEN

The edge of the forest was now the edge of the coming night. The road before them was still clearly visible; the bare dirt was lighter than the bough-strewn ground beneath the big pines. There, darkness was thickening, spreading as the shadows flowed together. The road had been empty since Yen and Jai had passed.

Equinox didn't even lay his ears back when the blond man whipped his horse and galloped past. Nothing interested the old mule now except getting back to his corral, his hay, and his ear rub from Colin. If he had any idea how scared his human passengers were, he gave no sign.

Anisett watched the blond man canter back toward them, then past, wheeling his horse around to ride behind the wagon. Anisett could hear him muttering, like a man lost in a fever dream. Most of what he said wasn't clear enough to understand, but Anisett could hear a few repeated phrases well enough. "This is my strike," he said over and over, sometimes looking up into the darkening sky as though it were a prayer.

No it isn't, Anisett thought. *It's mine and you are stealing it. And the best I can hope for is that no one gets killed.* Anisett's heart felt heavy, a weight inside her chest. Sooner or later the blond man would realize that his claim would be safe only with all of them dead—if he hadn't already. Was he crazy and desperate enough to kill them? Anisett closed her eyes, trying not to cry. If she had been less selfish, more cautious, this would not have happened.

"That's the turnoff up there?" The blond man spurred his horse alongside the wagon. Anisett's mother nodded. He looked up at the sky, gauging the diminishing light. "Then another mile or so to your cabin?" She nodded again. He fell silent as Equinox pulled the creaking wagon toward the turn.

"Here," the blond man said as they reached the little road that led to their cabin. His urgent voice startled Anisett. Did he think Anisett's mother might keep going on up to Veazie City, or Hamilton, or all the way to Bidwell's Bar? Anisett caught her breath. Why hadn't they lied to him about where their cabin was? They could have kept Equinox plodding all night long—by morning they would surely run into more wagons and coaches. Deeker's Creek Road joined the main road that ran along the Sacramento River seven or eight miles farther on. Anisett dug her fingernails into her palms. They should have thought of that. *She* should have.

Toby was watching her. She shook her head, trying to control her emotions. He patted her hand, then looked away. Colin was leaning against Anisett's side, and she looked down into his face. He appeared to be peaceful: a child who had simply gone to sleep on a long wagon ride.

Anisett's mother let the reins sag and sat back on the seat as they reached the crossroad. There was no reason to cue Equinox; he knew the way home. He rounded the corner slowly, the wagon jouncing across the ruts.

As Equinox plodded his way down the dusty little wagon track that ran to their cabin, Colin suddenly stretched and sat up. Anisett held her breath. Usually he was very calm after his withdrawals, but not always.

Colin looked at Toby and smiled, then scooted to the rear of the wagon where he could pat Toby's mare as they rolled along. The blond man watched him but said nothing. Equinox slowed a little as they started up the last hill.

"Whip the mule up," the blond man said suddenly. "If we get there before pitch dark, she could show me the creek." He gestured toward Anisett.

Anisett's mother turned. "We will not get there before it's too dark. It's too dark now."

The blond man looked around, squinting. He nodded reluctantly. "It wouldn't be if you had hurried a little." He dug his spurs into his horse's sides and rode forward, pulling his hat off to slap Equinox's hindquarters, whooping suddenly. Equinox broke into a resentful trot. He shook his harness, jingling the buckles. Anisett's mother let him slow down again after a few seconds. The blond man cursed, but she ignored him. Anisett felt a growing tenseness in her stomach.

When they turned into the cabin yard,

Equinox pulled the wagon past the door, then backed up without being guided. Toby's mare sidled and snorted but managed to maneuver with the wagon. Equinox stopped once he had pushed the wagon around, into the side yard where Anisett's mother left it every night. As Equinox lowered his head and waited, she set the brake and got down slowly. "Colin," she said carefully. "Go inside now."

"No, Rosa," the blond man contradicted her. "Let's keep everyone close. You," he nodded at Toby. "You get up on the porch now." He dismounted and wrapped his reins over the tie bar with his left hand; he was holding his revolver in his right. Anisett stared at it. If they could just make him drop the gun, maybe they could overpower him, all of them together. Or maybe one of them could get to Toby's horse and ride for help.

The blond man was silent, watching Toby climb out of the wagon and walk to the porch. He elevated the barrel of his gun slightly, following Toby's movement. "Just sit down there, on the steps." Toby sat. "You go sit next to him, you two." The blond man pointed at Anisett and Colin. "Your mama can unhitch this dog-meat mule."

Colin looked up sharply, then glanced at

Anisett. His eyes moved to Equinox, then back. Anisett shook her head. Colin was used to giving Equinox an ear scratch while their mother unhitched. If this had been a normal night, Anisett would already have been carrying the clean pails inside to get them soaking in soapy water.

Anisett exhaled slowly, longing for her usual work. If the blond man somehow went away without any of them getting hurt, she would never complain again. She would never wish for a different life or a brother who was smarter or who did more work. She would never care about gold again. *Please God*, she prayed. *Just protect us. I'll be good forever.* She sat next to Toby, smoothing her long skirt, tucking it close to her legs for warmth. The air was getting chilly.

Equinox suddenly tossed his head. Anisett stared at him. He rarely wasted effort on theatrics. He lifted his muzzle, taking in big, gulping breaths of the night air, then blowing it out in little whuffing spurts. He stared into the darkness, one ear pricked forward, the other straight back. He pawed at the ground.

"Colin," Anisett's mother said calmly, as though this was a common occurrence on an unremarkable evening. "Go scratch that mule's ears and calm him down." Before the blond man could object, Anisett's mother spun and in three quick steps was lifting Colin off the porch, nudging him toward Equinox's head.

The blond man glared at Anisett's mother. "I want him on the porch."

She looked over her shoulder as she went back to unbuckling the harness. "If this mule gets to braying, he won't stop until we all have headaches and every catamount in ten miles is on its way here to see what is stupid enough to make so much noise in the night." She impatiently snapped one of the trace fasteners, the leather popping sharply, like a distant gunshot. Equinox, lost in the pleasure of Colin's ear-scratching, did not move. "Maybe you don't care if mountain cats eat all the chickens and tear up the coop getting at them. But I certainly do." Anisett's mother slid the crupper over Equinox's tail, patting him gently as she worked.

"Just hurry with it," the blond man said. He glanced around, looking into the darkness in the direction Equinox had. Anisett followed his gaze. Toby's mare was standing quietly enough. There was nothing out there but pine trees.

"Where did you find it?" the blond man said, suddenly focusing on Anisett. His eyes looked too bright, shining with intensity in the lantern light.

Anisett made a vague gesture in the wrong direction. "Down there."

"In the creek bed? In the water?"

Anisett nodded hesitantly.

"Did you dig for it?"

Anisett shook her head, then regretted it. She should have told him it had taken weeks of digging to find the one little piece of gold. Maybe then the glitter in his eyes would go out. But it was too late. His face had lit with joy.

"Right on top? Some of the richest strikes have been that way. Right on top, like it was meant to be found."

Anisett didn't respond. She had overheard this kind of talk a hundred times in the mining camps. There were endless theories about where gold would be found and why.

"It could mean that it washed down from upstream, though," the blond man went on. Anisett glanced at her mother, who stood with her hands on Colin's shoulders, holding him still and quiet. The harness was off Equinox. It was time to put him in his corral for the night.

The blond man was muttering to himself, his eyes unfocused. "It could be deep. If it is, I'll just have to dig. I could find a partner or two. If Jim hadn't run off back to the states . . ." He bent to pick a burr from his trouser leg. When he straightened, Anisett's mother spoke quietly.

"We have to put the mule in his corral now."

The blond man answered. His voice was louder, harder. "Put the dog meat away, then. The boy's horse can go in with him."

Anisett's mother crossed the yard, leading Toby's mare. Colin led Equinox. The blond man moved off to one side to be able to cover them all with the gun. "Where's the lantern?" he demanded when they walked back across the yard toward him.

Colin was fiddling with a stem of hay from the corral. Anisett's mother hesitated, then spoke. "It's just inside the door. Left side, on a hook."

While the blond man opened the cabin door and stuck his head inside, Toby leaned to whisper in Anisett's ear. "My uncles will find us." Toby sat back just as the blond man stepped out of the doorway with the lantern in his hand.

Anisett nodded at Toby, the tiniest of motions, then looked off into the darkness again. He meant well, but he was wrong. No one was going to help them. Somehow, they had to help themselves.

The blond man had raised the lantern glass

and was now struggling to strike a match left-handed on the rough planks. He glanced up every few seconds. Suddenly, the match snapped in half. He cursed, and fished another from his pocket. His eyes flicked up at them again. Reassured that none of them had moved, he put his attention back on the match.

Anisett saw Toby watching intently. The blond man was still bent at the waist, striking impatiently at the planks with the new match. Toby began moving, as slowly as a clock hand, easing his weight forward. The second match snapped. It skittered over the planks, flaring once, then dropped off the edge of the porch into the dust, smoking. Cursing again, but without straightening up or looking around, the blond man set the revolver down close to his foot and dug his right hand into his shirt pocket. Toby was half standing now, poising himself, his eyes flickering from the blond man's face to the gun. Anisett held her breath.

The third match struck immediately, a miniature torch of flame springing to life. The blond man cursed again, this time in relief, and glanced up. Toby sat back down, an instant too late.

"Get up," the blond man snarled. "You want

to get up?" He had the revolver solidly in his hand again, and for a long, tense moment his breathing was ragged, his eyes hard and dark. "You ain't going to take this from me. My best friend died yesterday—he was all I had left in the world. Day before that I got a letter . . ." His voice trailed off, his eyes dimming. "Lila said she'd wait for me, but she married the dry goods store clerk."

"That's a common enough story here," Anisett's mother said softly, and there was pity in her voice. The blond man didn't answer her.

"You two"—he gestured abruptly at Toby and Anisett—"go in now. Startle me, or try anything at all, and I will shoot." He leveled the gun at Toby. "Don't doubt it for a second, boy."

Anisett glanced at the blond man's horse. Her mother's rifle stuck out of the scabbard. "Go on," the blond man ordered angrily. "Inside." Toby led the way and Anisett followed. They stood inside the door.

"And you, Rosa," the blond man prompted. "You and the little idiot." Anisett turned and saw Colin flinch. He didn't know what it meant, she was pretty sure, but he knew it was hateful.

Anisett felt something harden inside herself. The blond man might be grief stricken and crazy from destroyed hope. But he was also cruel. He herded Anisett's mother and Colin through ahead of himself, then brought up the rear, his gun held steadily on them as they went in.

The blond man set the lantern on the table, then looked around. "Better than the tents I have been living in for the past two years." He shook his head, and Anisett saw an odd expression in his eyes. "Maybe this can all work out. They said you're a widow. Maybe it doesn't have to be . . . like this." His voice faded but his intent was clear enough. He looked at Anisett's mother and she turned her head, staring at the wall. The blond man cursed softly.

In the yellowish light the cabin looked strange to Anisett, all its familiar warmth drained away by the man who stood tensely near the door.

CHAPTER TWELVE

The blond man had tied Toby up with kitchen twine—the same hemp cord her mother used for hanging chickens in the storeroom. It was strong and stiff. Then he forced Anisett's mother to sit on the edge of Colin's cot with Colin beside her. With everyone settled, he had gone through the cabin, tossing their clothing aside, searching their trunks for weapons. He had found one old pistol, rusted and ruined, that had belonged to Anisett's grandfather, and five big knives from the kitchen. These he had taken outside and thrown, one by one, into the trees at the edge of the yard.

Now that the cabin was safe, Anisett was to make coffee, then supper. She relit the stove fire and put on a pot of water to boil. She opened the coffee tin and scooped out a few tablespoons of the precious dark beans. She ground them in the mortar, careful to mash each bean into coarse grains without reducing them to paste. She glanced at the others. Her mother was pale, rocking Colin a little against her side. Toby's gaze was full of frustration and fury.

The blond man held the gun on Anisett, but loosely now, his hand relaxed. He waited, seemingly patient, as she boiled the coffee and brought it to him with a dish of sugar.

"I ain't had coffee in a long time," he murmured as she turned away. "I thank you kindly." He turned to smile at Anisett's mother. "I do appreciate this, Ma'am."

Anisett shivered, turning her back to hide the disgust on her face. He couldn't really think her mother could *like* him after everything he'd done? This sudden politeness was more frightening than anything.

Anisett filled a pot with water from the bucket and slid it onto the stove top, over the firebox, where it would boil fastest. Then she looked around the kitchen. It would be easiest just to boil up stew meat from the storeroom. Anisett's thoughts stopped. Fear and hope prickled over her skin. They never went outside the cabin at night. If they had to go to the storeroom, they used the hidden trapdoor beside her mother's bed. But tonight . . .

Involuntarily, Anisett glanced at the doeskin. A dozen plans whirled in her mind. They were all too complicated. The blond man would never stay outside long enough for any of them to work. And if he caught them trying to escape, he'd probably start shooting.

Anisett cleared her throat, an idea forming in her mind. "I need to go get stew beef." Her voice was so muted that she had to repeat it. She looked askance, afraid the hope in her heart would shine in her eyes and betray her. She risked a glance at Toby. He was watching the blond man.

"Go where?" The blond man's voice was suspicious, and she forced herself to look at him but could not answer.

"To the storeroom." Anisett's mother filled the silence. "It's on the back wall of the cabin; it's cooler out there for the meat."

The blond man narrowed his eyes. "Outside?"

Anisett nodded, trying to look impatient

instead of terrified, but again, her mother had to answer for her. "We can't hang a side of beef in here. The warmth from the stove would spoil it."

The blond man nodded slowly. Anisett felt herself exhale and realized she had been holding her breath. "I'll take a candle?" She didn't mean it to sound like a question, but it did.

The blond man arched his brows as though considering. "I suppose you'll need to see?" She nodded, then realized he was making fun of her. He had turned to face Anisett's mother. "Rosa? Would you have to go with her?"

Anisett's mother was so startled by the question that she blinked, tightening her grip on Colin's shoulder, obviously unsure how to answer. The blond man took off his hat and set it on the table next to the lantern. "There's not likely any danger out there?" His voice was quiet now, like that of a reasonable man trying to understand what the situation called for. Anisett's mother shook her head slowly, uncertainly.

"Then she won't need that rifle, will she?" the blond man asked easily. Anisett's mother lowered her eyes. He laughed, then stood up and walked to Toby, checking the twine that held his wrists and feet together. He straightened up, leveling the revolver at Anisett. "Get your candle."

Anisett crossed the room and got a candle from the box on the hearth. The ashes had been cleaned out of the fireplace—they never lit fires in the summer. The matchbox was on the mantle. Once the candle was burning, she looked up.

The blond man gestured with his revolver. "Ready?"

Anisett walked in front of him, shielding the candle with her left hand. Her breath came in quick little spasms. This could be their only chance. She had to do something. But what? The blond man opened the door. Anisett went out, surprised at the ink black sky. There was no moon at all.

The blond man walked to his horse and pulled the rifle free. Anisett hesitated. He stood with a revolver in his right hand and a rifle in his left, and he smiled at her. "Get going."

Anisett could scarcely breathe. Everything depended on his staying out on the porch—and staying calm. She stepped down into the yard. "Would you wait where you could hear if anything happened to me?" Anisett hoped he couldn't hear the shaking in her voice. "The dark scares me a little."

The blond man didn't answer immediately. Since he was silhouetted against the amber light of the doorway, she couldn't see his face. But when he did speak, his voice was flat. "I'll wait. But don't dawdle." He leaned the rifle against the wall of the cabin, to the right of the door. "If you run off, that brother of yours will pay for it."

Anisett took a deep breath and started around the house. The instant she was out of his sight, she ran, cupping her hand over the candle flame to keep it from blowing out. She could feel her pulse at the base of her throat, in her ears. Trembling, she lifted the bar on the storeroom door, pulling it open.

Once inside, Anisett moved even more swiftly. She turned the candle to drip wax on the wall niche, then stuck it into the little puddle as it hardened. There. Now it couldn't fall or go out. She grabbed the meat knife and cut strips of beef with frantic hurry. When she had enough, she set it on the pickle barrel, then spun around to raise the root cellar door. Now her real work began; if only she could do it quickly enough.

Without the candle, Anisett made her way through the root cellar and climbed the ladder that led to the trapdoor beside her mother's bed. She could feel time sliding past. How many minutes before he came looking for her? How many seconds?

Shaking, she lifted the trapdoor half an inch and listened. Nothing. Was the blond man still out on the porch? She raised the trapdoor a little more, as far as she dared, and slipped the meat knife through the crack, onto the cabin floor. She could feel the soft underside of the doeskin rug on the back of her hand. Barely breathing, she pushed the knife forward, then released it. She eased the trapdoor closed and clambered down the ladder, then whirled to run back through the root cellar. All she could do now is pray.

As she emerged from the cellar door into the storeroom, Anisett heard the blond man's voice. Her heart froze. Then she realized he was shouting at her; he was still on the porch. She scooped up the chunks of beef she had cut. She popped the candle free of the hardened wax that held it. Then she ran.

"It's about time," the blond man said roughly as she came around the corner of the cabin. He was standing tensely in the yard. "What took you so long?"

"The door was stuck," Anisett mumbled as she walked toward him. It sounded silly, but he seemed to accept it. Anisett slowed her step, trying to gain even a few extra seconds to think. She had to get inside the cabin before he did.

Across the dark yard, Equinox began to bray. It was a loud, grating sound, unpleasant and unnerving in the soft night air.

"Get clear," the blond man warned Anisett. He raised his revolver and pulled the hammer back with his thumb.

"No," she screamed. "Please don't!" The sound of her voice startled Equinox into silence.

"Anisett?" her mother shouted from inside. "What's wrong?"

"Nothing," the blond man yelled back. Then he lowered his voice and the revolver. "Come on."

Anisett came to a sudden decision. "I have to go start the stew," she said as evenly as she could, then whirled and bolted for the cabin door. The blond man shouted angrily behind her, but she ran as fast as she could, crossing the porch in two long strides.

"The meat knife is under the doeskin," Anisett whispered to her mother. She saw hope flare in her mother's eyes—and pride and love. A few seconds later, when the blond man came in the door, he saw her standing by the sideboard, cutting up the meat with the little paring knife.

Anisett could hear the blond man's boots on the plank floor, his spurs jangling as he paced back and forth, but she refused to turn and look at him. He began muttering to himself again as she got two onions out of the bin and set about making stew.

After a few minutes, the blond man stopped pacing. Anisett turned far enough to see him as she moved from the drain board back to the stove. He was standing silently in the doorway, turning the little piece of gold over and over in his left hand, glancing up every few seconds. He saw her looking and scowled. "Finish supper."

Anisett leaned away from the onion she was dicing and glanced across the room behind her. There was a wide wrinkle in the center of the doe-skin that stood a little higher than the others. Anisett looked at her mother, willing her to get ready. Her mother gave her a tiny nod.

"Would you hand me down that pot rag, please?" Anisett asked the blond man. She pointed. The rag was hanging above the cookstove on its hook. "I'm not tall enough." It was true, she had to stand on her tiptoes to reach it.

The blond man looked at her. "Pot rag?"

Anisett pointed again. He walked across the room, his back to the sleeping alcove. *Now*, Anisett thought silently, hoping her mother was alert. *Now!*

The blond man reached up to get the rag and

Anisett held her breath, every nerve in her body focused through her ears. There was no sound, no telltale clatter, no rustling of skirts. The blond man stepped back, looking at her as she thanked him. She pretended to stumble a little. He reached out and steadied her with his left hand, then turned to scan the room behind him.

Anisett resisted the impulse to turn around, too. Instead, she prayed. The blond man did not curse or shout. He went to stand near the door again. Anisett glanced at her mother and got one more almost invisible nod. She had the knife?

Listening to her own triumphant heart, Anisett used the rag to pad her palm and pulled the pot forward, then lifted the heavy iron lid. Setting it on the warming shelf above the stove, she scooped up the chopped meat and onions and dumped them into the boiling water. Then she replaced the lid and slid the pot to the rear again, where the fire was hottest. Only after that did she risk another quick look.

The wrinkle beneath the doeskin was gone. The rug lay flat and smooth against the planks again. Her mother had put her arms around Colin—his eyes were wide. Toby shot her a glance; then he looked down again.

Anisett turned back to the stew before the

blond man noticed. They had a chance now. A small chance, to be sure, but hope sang in her ears as she cooked. There were a few carrots still lying on the drain board from that morning. She began to peel them.

CHAPTER THIRTEEN

Anisett was setting bowls of stew around the table when Equinox began braying again. The blond man started, then straightened, pushing himself away from the door frame and turning to look out. Equinox kept it up, a noise loud enough to carry for a mile or more. The blond man spun the barrel of his pistol, checking the chambers, then cocked it.

"Don't hurt him," Colin blurted out.

Anisett's mother leaped up to stand in front of Colin. "Please. You can have the gold."

The blond man started toward her, his face set with fury. "It's already *mine*." He raised his left hand, but Anisett's mother stepped back and kept talking.

"Please. Just leave the mule alone. Leave us all alone and we'll help you. We'll—"

"Stop talking," the blond man roared at her. "Go sit down."

Anisett watched her mother come forward and position herself so that the blond man had to face away from Colin and Toby. She reached out and tried to take his hand. The blond man shook her off, stepping back and raising the pistol once more. Out of the corner of her eye, Anisett saw Colin move, saw a flash of bright metal. Her heart nearly stopped. Colin had the knife? Then she saw him crouch beside Toby. If the blond man happened to turn now . . .

Anisett forced herself to step forward. "Equinox hasn't done anything," she argued. Her voice was shaking with fear, but she didn't allow herself to think about the pistol or about anything at all except the need to keep the blond man turned away from her brother and Toby. "How can you even think about hurting a poor mule? How can you?"

The blond man shoved at her, knocking her

sideways. Anisett's mother stepped forward again, at an angle that forced the blond man to turn again to face her. "How dare you push my daughter?" Her chin was high, her eyes intense. Anisett could see her mother's fear, and her courage. She was talking so loudly that no other sound could penetrate. The blond man had raised the pistol and was pointing it at her, but she did not back down. Anisett knew why. If the blond man saw what Colin was doing, he *would* start shooting. Anisett's mother stepped back, still shouting. "How dare you? You have no right here. . . ."

Anisett eased her way behind the blond man. She picked up the stew ladle and filled it from the pot. Equinox had paused, but now he started up again, as though he could sense the struggle going on inside the cabin.

The blond man turned, and Anisett saw his face go white and rigid. "Get away from each other," he ordered Colin and Toby. He brought the pistol up, and Anisett stepped close behind him. She poured the near-boiling stew down his back.

The blond man screamed with pain from the scalding liquid soaking his skin and shirt, jerked the pistol upward, and turned a circle, swearing ferociously. In that instant, Toby came across the room. Red-faced, the blond man regained his footing and leveled the pistol. He fired, and Toby's whole body jerked as he collapsed, then lay still on the floor. Colin's wail of fear echoed the awful crack of the gunshot.

"Get out," Anisett's mother shouted to take the blond man's attention from Colin. Anisett stood frozen as the blond man turned toward her mother, rage in his eyes, the revolver shining in the lantern light. Anisett was terrified, but she did not allow herself to take her eyes off the gun. She raised the heavy ladle in her right hand and struck downward with every ounce of strength she possessed. The blond man screamed, and the revolver clattered to the floor. Anisett kicked it, sending it spinning across the smooth planks.

The blond man stood, breathing violently, holding his wrist. He was staring at the gun. Anisett's mother started past him. He shoved her backward and she clung to his arm, slowing him, but she wasn't strong enough to hold him. He shook her off and she fell heavily. Anisett cried out, then heard the blond man's curse. She looked up and her heart constricted.

Colin had picked up the revolver. For a second, he tried to hold it steady, pointing it at the blond man. Then he whirled and ran to the woodstove. Before the blond man could stop him, he had opened the firebox door and flung the pistol far back into the flames. The blond man slapped Colin aside and bent to stare through the little iron door at the stove fire. He stood again and looked around wildly, obviously searching for something he could use to reach into the flames. Colin stood transfixed, his eyes round with terror. The blond man was inching toward the door.

"The rifle!" Toby yelled, his voice pinched with pain.

Snake-quick, the blond man reached out and grabbed Colin. Anisett watched helplessly as he dragged her brother backward, toward the cabin door. Anisett's mother was sitting up, blinking, rubbing her cheek, pale and frightened. She suddenly seemed small.

Anisett forced herself to remain still until the blond man had passed through the door. Then she flew at the cot, lifting the edge, running her hands beneath the mattress and pillow. Frantic, she lifted one edge of the quilt, and the meat knife fell to the floor. She grabbed it up and ran for the door.

The blond man cursed violently. "You put the

rifle somewhere," he screamed at her, jerking Colin backward. "Where?"

"Not her," a calm voice said from behind them. "I move rifle."

The blond man spun around, pulling Colin with him. There, by the corral, stood Yen. Anisett almost cried out in relief. The blond man cursed again, almost in a whisper. Then he raised his voice. "Chinaman, I have no quarrel with you."

"I have quarrel with you," Yen replied. He lifted the rifle. "You hurt my friends." Anisett slipped off the porch and into the darkness while the blond man was facing Yen. The handle of the knife felt impossibly big and clumsy in her hand.

Colin was wrestling, trying to free himself, but the blond man was far too strong. "Yen!" Anisett heard her mother's voice at the door. "Don't shoot! You could hurt Colin." Behind her, Anisett could see Toby on the floor. His shirt was red with seeping blood.

"Don't come any closer," the blond man hissed. He tightened his grip on Colin, locking one arm around his neck.

Anisett worked her way forward, grateful now that there was no moon. "It's my gold," the blond man said quietly. Anisett wasn't sure that anyone heard him besides herself. He began muttering again, about all the wrongs done against him. Anisett heard Lila's name in the stream of words. She held the knife tighter. Maybe he had worked as hard as he said, maybe he had lost his sweetheart and his friend. It didn't matter. Nothing gave him the right to do this. She closed her eyes and prayed that Colin would be all right—that they would all be all right. Then she tucked her skirt into her waistband and began to crawl toward the blond man.

"You ain't going to shoot me, Chinaman," the blond man said, starting to work his way toward the side of the cabin where his horse was tied. "You could hit the boy."

Anisett heard her mother say something to Toby. Then she heard Yen asking what to do next. She felt the sting of tears behind her eyes and fought them, crawling faster. If the blond man made it to his horse, he might take Colin with him.

Trembling as she got close, Anisett raised the knife. She held her breath, then lunged forward, bringing the blade straight down as hard as she could. The blond man screamed as it cut his boot and pierced his skin. Anisett leaped to her feet and grabbed Colin. She ran, half pulling, half dragging him, back toward the glow of lantern light that spilled from the cabin door.

Breathing hard, still gripping the knife, Anisett stood on the porch, her arm around Colin's shoulders. Anisett's mother was holding the rifle now. Yen was behind the blond man, using his own lariat to tie his hands. Anisett looked back into the cabin. Toby was sitting up, his hand against his side. Colin ran to him. Anisett followed.

"I looked," Toby said in an astonished voice. "It didn't go in. It's just a real deep scratch and bloody. It hurts like fire," he added, trying to stand up. He sank back down. "I feel a little dizzy." Colin put his arms around Toby. Jai appeared in the doorway.

"I am so sorry. My father made me to sit in the wagon." She smiled her tiny smile and went into the kitchen.

Jai and Anisett washed Toby's wound and bound it with a strip of cloth torn from an old sheet. Outside, Anisett could hear her mother and Yen talking about what to do next. Without meaning to, Anisett began to cry. Colin hugged her. Toby held her hand. Jai sat close by. This time, Anisett let the tears come.

Toby's uncles came at dawn when they could follow the wagon tracks to the cabin. They made a fuss over Mother, Colin, and me, and asked if we would consider them as partners. Mother says it is up to me. Toby's uncles said the miners will have a trial and banish the blond man. No one knows his name and he would not speak or answer anyone's questions before they took him away to Schalt's. That's where they will have the miners' meeting. I am glad they will make him leave California. I never want to see him again. I wish I could forget his ice blue eyes.

I wonder what will happen when we dig for gold. I hate to imagine a tent camp spreading down the valley, and it might. But gold could mean a special tutor for Colin, a better house and someday, cattle and horses for the ranch. My father's dream may come true. I talked to Mother about it last night. She says she will consider staying now.

Day before yesterday I didn't know who I could trust. I do now. Toby and his uncles and Yen and his family will help us dig for gold. They were all willing to risk themselves to help us. And even if we find no more gold *at all—we have found friends. My mother says she is proud of me, that I was very brave. If I can grow to be half as brave as she, I will be happy.*